DARE TO BE SCANDALOUS

LEAGUE OF UNWEDDABLE GENTLEMEN, BOOK 3

TAMARA

COPYRIGHT

PROLOGUE

1826 London

*W*illow raced up her aunt's stairs, having been summoned back from her daily ride at Hyde Park. Sweat pooled on her brow, and she could feel it running down the line of her back beneath her gown. It was too soon. This day could not be the end of her aunt.

She ran as fast as her riding ensemble would allow and pushed open her aunt's bedroom door, coming to an abrupt halt at the sight of her lady's maid, the butler, and housekeeper, all of their faces masks of pity and sadness.

"Auntie?" She came and sat on the bed beside her, reaching for her hands. They were cold and limp in hers, and Willow squeezed them a little, needing to rouse her, keep her with her for just a bit of time longer.

"I'm still here, my child. I waited for you."

Tears pooled in Willow's eyes, and she clasped her aunt, her only family left in the world into an embrace, her throat as raw as if a hot poker had pierced her there, making each breath painful and hard.

1

"I'm so sorry. I went riding. I did not know that you were so poorly."

Her aunt shushed her, the action bringing on another bout of coughs that wheezed and rattled her chest. The hack sounded painful, and if her aunt's grimace each time she coughed was any indication, the infection was causing discomfort.

"I want you to go riding, even when I'm gone. You will have more time on your hands then. You won't have to trundle after me anymore."

That may be so, but Willow would have to trundle after someone. When her aunt passed, she would need to find employment, and soon. The thought brought her no pleasure, and her stomach churned at the prospect she would not find work. Not that her friends would leave her out on the street, but they had their own lives now, families to take care of, they did not need a friend latching on to them for charity.

"Never mind that," she said, not wanting to talk about what she would do after her aunt passed. The doctor had promised she had some weeks left, not one. Her decline had been so fast in the last few days. Too fast. Willow prayed for time to stop. For her aunt not to leave her alone in this world. "You'll be better soon, and we'll look back on this day and laugh. You'll see. Nothing to fear just yet."

Her aunt's lips twisted into a grin. "I wanted to tell you before I go what I've done." Her aunt squeezed her hands, suddenly stronger and capable as they once were. "You will have time, my dear. To finally do as you wish because I'm leaving you everything that I have. The London townhouse, my estate in Kent, my money. All of it is yours."

Willow stared at her aunt, knowing full well her mouth was gaping. "You cannot. I'm not a Vance."

"No one is. With no children and no one to take on the title, I can do what I wish with everything else. The title and house in Norfolk will revert to the Crown, but nothing else."

"Are you sure, Auntie?" Willow asked. Surely there was more entailed than just the Norfolk property. She could not get everything.

"I will lose the house in Norfolk, but everything else is yours, my darling." Her aunt sat up a little, her eyes bright. "You have been a shining light in my world since Maurice died, the child that I never had. You are my sister's daughter, but you are mine as well. I want you to be safe, to be protected after I'm gone. Making you my heir accomplishes all this. I will rest easy knowing you will be protected."

"Oh, Auntie." Willow's vision blurred at her impossibly good fortune at a time when the loss of the woman before her would be too much to bear. "I love you so much. Thank you. It is too much."

Her aunt sighed, lying back on the bedding, a small smile about her lips. "I'm happy to." She reached up, touching Willow's cheek with her palm. "You will suit being an heiress, just try and keep some of the funds for yourself and not give it away to all the unfortunates. I know what a good heart you have."

Willow chuckled. Even now, as ill as her aunt was, she was making banter, trying to make her laugh. "I will try. I promise." Willow sat back as her aunt slumped into her bedding, her eyes closing with the exertion of having spoken the last few minutes.

She watched her, holding her hand. Her chest rose and fell, telling Willow she was still here. "I will miss you so much, Auntie. Thank you for loving me as you did. I will never forget your kindness."

The housekeeper came over to Willow and placed a comforting hand on her shoulder. Willow could not stop looking at her aunt's breathing. In. Out. In. Out. In. She waited for the exhale. It never came. Willow stood, clutching at her aunt's hand. "Auntie. Auntie," she cried, louder this time, but nothing. No breaths. No words. Nothing.

She turned to the housekeeper who stared at her, tears in her own old eyes. "She's gone to be with God, my dear. Come away now."

Willow did as they bade, unable to fathom what had just happened. Her aunt could not be gone. It wasn't possible. She paused at the threshold of the room, looking back at her only relative — the dearly departed sister to her mama. The Viscountess Vance. "I will miss you," she whispered, before leaving the room. "Always."

CHAPTER 1

Twelve months later — The Season

*A*braham Blackwood, Marquess Ryley, Abe to his friends and those who were fortunate enough to bed him, watched as his mistress energetically sucked and licked with enthusiasm on his phallus, her chocolate-brown hair cascading over his legs and tickling him with each movement. He leaned back in his chair, enjoying the slide of her tongue, the massaging of his tight, aching balls with her hand. She was a clever minx, and one he doubted he'd ever tire of — worth every jewel and penny he spent on her.

"Fuck, that's good." She made a sweet mewling sound that throbbed up his spine. He was close, could feel his balls tightening with his impending release. Lottie increased her ministrations as if sensing he was near spilling into her mouth. Another perfect reason he had her as his mistress. She encompassed good sense and was a fucking hot shag. She shifted a little, taking him to the back of her throat, and his seed released, hard and long into her mouth. The perfectionist and expert that she was, she swallowed, not spilling any over her swollen, pinkened lips.

"Hmm, delicious," she purred, sitting up on his desk and spreading her legs. He raised one brow, taking in her wet cunny. "You've been busy down there."

"Do you like it? It's all the rage in Paris. I thought it might be fun," she said, glancing down at her clean-shaven quim.

He licked his lips, not minding either way. Shaved or not, he enjoyed eating a woman to release.

A series of knocks sounded on the door.

Lottie sighed, lying back on the desk.

Abe reached out, running his finger along her wet folds, rolling his thumb over her sweet nubbin. "Fuck off," he yelled, kissing her inner thigh.

"It's me, Whitstone," came a muffled voice from the other side of the wood.

Abe groaned, settling back in his chair and watching as Lottie, aware that their playtime was over, shuffled off the desk and adjusted her clothing. "I'll meet you upstairs shortly. Be ready," he said, as she threw him a mischievous grin over her shoulder before opening his library door to reveal Whitstone, arm raised as if to knock again.

"Come in." Abe gestured to one of his oldest friends since Eton. Whitstone had protected him when other boys at the school would poke fun at his mama, a Spanish woman who had been fortunate enough to marry Marquess Blackwood when he was touring the continent. The young marquess had returned to England with a wife. Quite the scandal considering she wasn't a perfect English rose, as the marquess was expected to wed.

"My friend," Whitstone said, smiling at Lottie as she

walked past His Grace, running her finger across the duke's chest.

Abe laughed. Cheeky wench.

Whitstone entered the room, closing the door. "I apologize if I interrupted you," he said, smirking.

"Drink?" Abe asked, standing and going to the decanter to pour a glass of whiskey.

"No, thank you. I have come here to ask for a favor and have little time. Otherwise, I would."

Abe raised his brow, downing his whiskey before pouring another. "What is it that you need?" He had little to do with society, not after what happened the last time he trod the boards at Almacks. Not that he'd ever be admitted to the place again, not after receiving a life ban for punching Lord Perfect, as he termed Lord Herbert, for being an ass. Something the man was afflicted with often.

"I'm not sure if you know Ava's good friend, Miss Willow Perry, but she's hosting a masquerade ball, a celebration to be back in society after the death of her aunt. She's become an heiress you see, worth over one hundred thousand pounds, and I want you there to keep her safe from those who may be looking at her as a bit of blunt to clear their debts. Ava is determined that Willow will marry for love and nothing else. Although…" Whitstone said, his tone bemused. "I'm not sure Willow thinks the same as the duchess."

Abe's lips twitched, well believing that what the duchess may think is well and good for her friend may not be what the lady in particular wants. The duke's wife could sometimes be, in every sense, a duchess used to getting what she wanted.

"You want me to babysit Miss Perry."

Whitstone leaned back in his chair, folding his legs.

"You make it sound like a chore. Duncannon will be there also, and myself. We'll make a good night of it, but we must keep her safe from blackguards that may seek to ruin her to gain her inheritance."

Abe rubbed a hand over his jaw, the prickle of whiskers reminding him that he'd not shaved this morning. "What if she wants a little rendezvous in the garden? Are we to stop her from having a little fun?" Abe had fun often with the ladies of the *ton* who were free from the marital bed or looking to cuckold it.

Whitstone raised his brow, his visage one of censure. "She's a lady, Ryley. She will not be looking for a quick tup on the lawn."

His lips twitched, knowing how very fun a quick fuck up against a trellis or terrace railing could be. There was nothing sweeter than lifting the skirts of a willing woman and sliding into the tight quim that wrapped and pulled you in until you were lost. He thought about what Whitstone asked. There would be many women there, plenty of willing ladies under disguise for the masked ball who may be up for a little fun with the Spanish Scoundrel.

"Very well. I'll attend. When is it?" he asked, sitting back behind his desk. He had a masquerade outfit that would suit his heritage and, most certainly, his dark character.

"Tomorrow evening. Miss Perry is living in the late Viscountess Vance's residence on Hanover Square. That was her aunt."

Abe stilled at the mention of the name Vance. The surname raising ire and regret in his veins. Not regret that her ladyship had passed or that he'd not paid his last respects, but that he'd not been able to make the woman pay for her dealings with his sweet mama. Viscountess

Vance had ensured his mother had never been accepted into society, helped along with Lord Perfect's mother too. A mean feat since his mother was a marchioness and much higher on the social ladder than lady Vance. Vance, however, had one thing that his mother never did.

English blood.

That this Viscountess Vance had a niece he'd not known of... Or perhaps he had, but had not paid enough attention when she'd been standing right under his nose.

"The night that we caught up with Mr. Stewart and threw the bastard into Newgate. That is where I've heard of Miss Perry. She was a school friend of the duchesses and Miss Evans. She was at your home that night, waiting with Ava and Hallie."

The duke nodded, sitting forward to lean on his knees. "They were all at a finishing school together in France. Madame Dufour's Refining School for Girls."

The duke took him in a moment, a small frown forming on his brow. Abe schooled his features, not wanting his friend to know of his loathing of the Vance family. Miss Perry's family.

"You seem curious about Miss Perry all of a sudden. You are going to behave yourself, aren't you, Ryley? Ava will tan my hide if you hurt Miss Perry in any way."

Abe chuckled, masking his features. No one knew how many nobs in London, how many families he'd paid back over the years for the wrong they did to his mama. Made her an outcast of society. Made her leave him and her life here in England to return to Spain. At least she was still living, and he saw her as often as he could. His father had never forgiven her for running away, and his sire had loathed her until his death only a few years ago.

A wasted life. For both of them. And he could lay it all

at the door of Viscountess Vance and Lady Herbert, Lord Perfect's mother and their wicked tongues.

"You forget that I have a mistress and have zero tolerance for society." The gaming den, Hells Gate, was profitable and diverting, and he sought out society little. Unless he stumbled across a willing lady in his club, a woman looking for a little diversion, only then was he up to being distracted, normally under her skirts.

Whitstone sighed, his shoulders sagging in relief. "Very good, you've put my mind at ease. So," he said, standing and clapping his hands. "Eight tomorrow night, Belgrave Square. Don't be late."

Abe stood and walked Whitstone to the door. "I'll not be late. You can count on me." He saw his friend out to his carriage and then started upstairs. He had a mistress to please, and he could use a little entertainment. No matter what he'd said to his friend, he would seek revenge on the late Viscountess's niece. If she were the last one in her ladyship's family that he could pay back, then she would be the one to suffer the consequences of her aunt's actions.

Abe frowned at his thoughts. His friendship with Whitstone and Duncannon was solid, but even he didn't know if it would survive his next step into society.

Certainly, Miss Willow Perry would not, that he was certain.

CHAPTER 2

*E*verything was in order for the masquerade. Willow had a team of servants working for her, ordering flowers, polishing the floor, cleaning windows, and ensuring the gardens were manicured and well-lit for the dance.

After returning to London she had made some changes to her life. Being an heiress allowed her certain freedoms she'd not had before. She had hired a companion, a widow who had a lenient mindset and liked nothing more than to read and keep to herself most days, allowing Willow to do as she wanted. Her two best friends, Evie and Molly, whom she had invited to London for the duration of the Season and beyond if they wished were also in attendance.

The house was certainly big enough for all of them, and with Miss Sinclair watching over them all, when she wasn't reading or strolling the gardens, the arrangement was perfect.

Willow stood at the ballroom doors, watching as the finishing touches were fitted to the room. She'd wanted the night to represent magic and mayhem. Flower decorations sat on every available surface, rich pinks, and stunning, white forget-me-nots that showered the area with sweet scents. Groupings of candles, each of different sizes, sat in corners, and the three chandeliers were currently lowered, footmen and housemaids ensuring new beeswax candles were installed. Sheer netting hung over the curtains and across the ceiling, giving the room an other-worldly feel. A world where she was the master of her own fate. A heady feeling indeed.

"Oh my, Willow. This room is beautiful!" Evie said, walking into the space and twirling. Molly joined her, looking up at all the flowers and decorations her servants had been busy putting up the last three days.

Pride filled her, and Willow smiled. "I couldn't agree more. My staff have outdone themselves. I will be sure to congratulate them with a glass of champagne. They will enjoy that I should think."

"I think they would very much," Molly said, joining her. "I cannot wait for the ball. I've never been to a masquerade before."

"Neither have I," put in Evie, her eyes bright with excitement. "With Ava and Hallie with us, it'll be like old times."

"Except they'll have their husbands with them," Molly said, a little put out by that fact. "But then you never know what friends they will bring. Perhaps by the end of the Season we'll all have husbands."

Evie beamed at the idea. Willow smiled. After losing her parents so young in her life, she wanted nothing more than to have a family of her own. Her aunt had been her last blood relative, and now that she was gone, there was no one. A husband would be a suitable travel companion, assist her in seeing Paris or Rome. Give her what she truly longed for—a child.

Willow, Evie, and Molly were the youngest of their friend set, and at seven and twenty, their time to find husbands was fast running out. The *ton* would have firmly placed them on the shelf and marked them as little or no consequence.

"I've ordered baths for you later today, and I've assigned you each a lady's maid to help you dress and have your hair styled. I hope you do not mind."

Evie gasped, clutching her arm so hard Willow thought it might stop the blood from flowing to her hand. "You've saved us both from another dreary year in the countryside with our families. As much as we love them, nothing ever happens in Oxfordshire or Hertfordshire."

Evie nodded. "The most exciting thing to occur in our village is church on Sunday. My brother has already laid bets at the local tavern on how long it will take for the vicar's new wife to fall asleep during her husband's sermon. His first wife, God rest her soul, was within seven to nine minutes, but this new one doesn't seem to have any stamina. We're guessing under five will be her limit."

Willow chuckled. "Come, I've had tea and sandwiches brought into the drawing room downstairs for lunch. I thought something a little informal would be nice. It has been so long since we've seen each other. At least a year."

"For me, yes," Evie said. "I had not seen you since Ava's Season-opening ball last year."

"Longer for me." Molly twined her arm with Willow's as they walked to the staircase to head up to the drawing room upstairs. "I've not been to town for a good two years at least. As you know, my parents are not in favor of London and so like to keep us hidden away in the country. Did you know that Mama tried to push me toward a local farmer as a potential husband? Under normal circumstances, I would gladly marry a farmer should I be in love with him, but he was my father's age. I could not countenance it. When I received your letter, dear Willow, I could not come soon enough."

"We're going to have so much fun," Willow interjected. "The chaperone I hired, Miss Sinclair, is, well, let me just say, a little flippant and inclined to forget her duties, so there will be plenty of opportunities to explore every part of this city, and the entertainments it has on offer."

"Like the gambling den, Hell's Gate," Evie supplied, a mischievous twinkle in her gaze. "Everyone is talking of it."

"Exactly like Hell's Gate," Molly said, smirking.

Willow frowned, having never heard of the club. "What is Hell's Gate? It sounds less than respectable."

"That's because it is," Evie said.

They came to the drawing room and entering the large, well-lit space, Willow couldn't help but be proud of her home. The windows that ran floor to ceiling lit the room with natural light, giving it a warm and homely feel. Willow closed the door. A tea service sat on a small table beside the settee. Her butler waited at its side.

"I'll serve the tea. That will be all, thank you, Thomas," Willow said, not asking what else her friends knew of this club until they were alone. Once the door closed, Willow set about pouring them all tea and handing each of them a sugar cookie.

"Now, tell me more of the club and, more importantly, how you know of it."

Evie waved Molly's curiosity aside. "Well, I'm surprised

you do not. Remember when Hallie had all that trouble with Mr. Stewart? Well, he was caught at the Hell's Gate. The Bow Street runner found him there after the owner alerted the investigator that Mr. Stewart was a regular customer."

"Who is the owner?" Willow asked. She remembered the situation well with their dear friend Hallie, but she had not heard how it all went about that the would-be murderer Mr. Stewart was caught.

"That's the delicious part," Evie interjected. "It's Marquess Ryley. He owns the club, has done so for years. I heard Ava talking to Whitstone about it all, that's how I know. The Marquess is by all account quite wild, but a friend of Whitstone and Duncannon's, ever since Eton from what I understand."

How very interesting. Willow poured her tea, seating herself across from her friends. "And Mr. Stewart was caught at this club. I remember the night all of that occurred. I was with Ava and Hallie at Ava's London town-house." Vaguely Willow remembered seeing the men return that night, two familiar, one who was not. The one she'd not known had been dark as night, his hair ebony and disheveled as if he'd been woken from slumber. She remembered her breath had caught at the sight of him. Never had she seen anyone who looked as wicked as he did. As for his reaction to her, there was very little. His glance had slid over her as if she were not even there. Most disappointing. "What is it that happens at this club?" Willow queried.

"Well, as to that," Molly said, "anything that you want. Or at least, whatever a man wants. Gambling, dining, dancing, and of course, the fairer sex can ply their trade if you know what I mean..."

Willow raised her brow. "And a marquess runs such an establishment?"

"Oh yes, he's known in London as the Spanish Scoundrel. I'm surprised you've never seen him."

"Actually, I believe I may have, but I wasn't aware of his reputation or who he was. We were not introduced."

"Maybe not so surprising, he's a little wild. I would think Duncannon and Whitstone would try and keep their wives' friends at a safe distance from the gentleman. He's as wicked as they come, and cares little to the fact."

Even more interesting. Willow could do with a little excitement in her life, and perhaps Lord Ryley would be a diversion to kick off her first London Season as an independent heiress. "I've invited Whitstone and Duncannon to the ball this evening. I wonder if they will extend the invitation to their friend. What a coup my masquerade will be if Lord Ryley makes an appearance."

"He's very handsome. I'm sure if he deigns to wear a masque or not, you will recognize him immediately. Few would not," Evie put in, picking up another sugar cookie and taking a healthy bite.

Molly nodded. "Oh, I'm so excited about this evening. We cannot thank you enough, Willow, for giving us this opportunity to be here in London with you. We shall treasure our time in town with you forever."

"You're more than willing to stay for as long as you like. I'm not going anywhere, and if my newfound circumstances enable you to make grand matches yourself, then I will be well pleased. As for myself, I'm open to a little flirtation and courting if a gentleman so chooses." Willow smiled at her friends as more ideas for their life floated into her mind. "And if we become bored with London, or a husband is not forthcoming, next year we can always travel abroad, to Paris, Madrid or Rome. We can do whatever we like."

Evie slumped back into her chair, sighing. "That sounds wonderful. You're too good to us, Willow. We will never be able to repay you your kindness."

"You do not need to repay me anything. Had my aunt not bestowed on me her fortune, I should be at this very moment seeking employment as a companion. If with this new life that's been bestowed on me, I can make the lives of my friends easier, then I shall. This house is too big for me to be rattling around in alone in any case. Too many years it's been empty, without balls and parties, laughter and fun. I want us to bring all of that back and enjoy ourselves as much as we can."

"That sounds like a most perfect plan," Molly said, her gaze wistful. "And it all starts tonight with the masquerade. What fun we shall have. I can hardly wait."

"Ava and Hallie said they would arrive earlier than their husbands, to ensure everything was in place. We shall all have such a wonderful time, and be all back together again." The clock on the mantle struck the second hour, reminding Willow of how late the afternoon was getting and the time required to prepare for a masquerade ball. "We should be going upstairs soon. We have so much to do yet before this evening. If you wanted to rest before our early dinner, that might be wise. I believe the ball may go all night."

Evie rose from her chair. "You're right, we best not dawdle. Come on, ladies, let's be off. We have a mask to attend."

Willow followed her friends from the room, taking one last look in on the ballroom before heading upstairs. It was simply stunning and would be a night she was sure would be talked about for weeks to come. A perfect way to start the Season and to tell the world that Miss Willow Perry is no longer the meek, biddable niece of Viscountess Vance, but an heiress and a woman who's ready to live and enjoy all that life throws her way.

CHAPTER 3

*A*s society started to make their way into Willow's magic- and mayhem-themed ballroom later that evening, she was delighted to hear the gasps and exclamations as to its beautiful decoration. Her staff was to be commended, and she would ensure they had their glass of champagne, just as she promised them.

Willow stood between her friend, the Duchess of Whitstone and Countess Duncannon. Evie and Molly were already out dancing with two gentlemen who wore masks to cover their features. Willow had thought it would be easier to guess who some of the guests were, but it was proving more difficult than she'd first thought. Not that it mattered, only those who had produced their invitation were allowed entrance. Those who danced and enjoyed the festivities were an acquaintance of hers in some way or another. They were among friends.

"I must tell you, Willow before my maddening husband arrives, and you see for yourself," Hallie said, glancing at her. Hallie wore a golden mask, her dark hair perched high on her head in a motif of curls, an elegant gold chain running throughout the design. She had come as Athena, the goddess of wisdom and war. With her spear and shield, she looked as formidable as the goddess Willow imagined.

"Good gracious, whatever has Duncannon done now?" Willow asked, teasing her friend. It was very odd that his lordship would do anything against his wife, but something told Willow he might have this evening.

"Besides the fact he was determined to come tonight dressed as a servant to please his goddess, he is also bringing a friend that I've only ever met just once. And while I'm sure his lordship will be on best behavior, he is a little bit scandalous from all accounts."

Was she talking of Lord Ryley? The Spanish Scoundrel? Excitement thrummed in her veins that it could be so. "Who is to attend?" she asked.

"Abraham Blackwood, Lord Ryley. He's a marquess, and from all accounts, his name of scoundrel suits him well."

Better and better. "Evie and Molly told me a little of him this afternoon. He seems quite the gentleman," she teased. "Has he arrived? I would like to meet this Lord Ryley." To see for herself if all the fuss over this one man was worth it. Certainly, having a scandalous lord at her mask would create a little stir.

"They should not be long," Hallie said, glancing toward the ballroom doors. "Arthur was going directly to pick up Whitstone. Lord Ryley was already at our home when I left, so I should imagine they will all arrive very shortly." At the sound of tittering, an excited whisper went through the throng of guests. "Ah, they've arrived," Hallie said, a small smile playing about her lips as she glanced in the direction of her husband.

Willow's heart skipped a beat as she took in the sight of

Marquess Ryley. Well, her friends were undoubtedly not lying or embellishing the gentleman's charms. He had many—too many—possibilities of wickedness to count on two hands.

He was all darkness, his hair as black as the domino that he wore. His skin was sun-kissed, his eyes intelligent and assessing as he took in the room. People looked at the three powerful lords who had arrived, some giving them a wide berth as they passed them by.

Out the corner of her eye, she saw Ava wave to her husband, the duke, who spying her, turned to the other two gentlemen before they started in their direction. Everything within Willow stilled as those obsidian eyes settled on her, running over her face before dipping to her bodice. Heat prickled under her gown, and Willow had the urge to go outside to cool off a little.

The gentlemen joined them, and the duke made the introductions. Willow dipped into a curtsy and stood back as the duke and viscount asked their wives for a waltz. Willow watched as her friends, with their grand loves, moved out onto the ballroom floor, making a concerted effort to keep from looking at the marquess beside her. All six foot something of looming muscle that he was.

"I must offer you my condolences on the passing of your aunt, Miss Perry."

His voice was made for sin, or at least it pulled forth all the ideas of debauchery and everything one could do with a person such as the marquess. Deep and husky and like nothing she'd ever heard before. Willow glanced at him, her stomach fluttering as if a million butterflies were in there. He was watching her, and she sucked in a calming breath.

"Thank you, my lord. My aunt is greatly missed."

21

"Hmm," he said, and nothing else.

Willow narrowed her eyes at the noncommittal *hmm* and fought to come up with something else to say. The man was too overbearing, made her nervous, and yet she could not understand why. They shared mutual friends, he was a gentleman, even if he did not venture out into society all that much. The realization struck her as odd.

"I did not think you enjoyed such events, my lord. My understanding is that you very rarely enter society nowadays."

A muscle worked in his jaw, and her attention fixated on it. He had a lovely jaw, cutting and with the smallest shadow of stubble. Although she could not see all his features due to his mask, she could just make out high cheekbones, and his nose was perfect too, even if those eyes were as hard to read as a book with no words.

"I do not, but I have very persuasive friends as you well know." That was undoubtedly true. Willow knew that as well as anyone. Her friends had demanded they stay nearby during this ball to ensure her security. Now that she was an heiress, it made her more susceptible to men of little morals and even lesser fortunes.

Willow shook her head at the absurdness of it all. As if overnight, she had lost the ability to see suitors for who they were. If they were not interested in her before she gained her fortune, they should not bother with her now. She would marry for love and nothing less. With her newfound freedom, she could take the time to find a gentleman who loved her, shared similar pursuits, and wanted a family as she did.

"I understand well, but whatever would we do without them?" she said, making light of his words.

"Hmm," he said again, and she wondered if he had

any other vocabulary when answering her. They stood there for several minutes, neither speaking and with each moment that passed, Willow looked to see if any alternate friends were about that she could talk to. The marquess may like solitude and be a man of few words, but Willow was not.

"I understand you own a gentleman's club, my lord, and that you spend most of your time there. I hear it's very popular with the gentlemen of your set."

His all-too-penetrating gaze landed on her. Willow looked up at him, oddly wanting to know more about him and what he did. She'd never met a man who owned such a business, and her time in society this year was to explore and learn, to see and do more things while searching for a husband.

"Pray tell me, Miss Perry, how do you know about my business?"

"Hmm, well," she said, using his elusive response that was really no response at all, "It's our mutual friends again, I'm afraid. They told me, as well as a few other snippets of information."

He raised his brow, his lips twitching. Had she amused him? A little light of hope bloomed inside her that she had. He was so very severe, dangerous looking. It would not hurt him to smile. Willow could imagine how very sexy a slow-forming smile would be on his lips. What it would feel like to be the recipient of such a gesture. To have those lips on hers. A shiver stole down her spine, and she pushed the thought aside, wondering where it came from.

"So you know what society calls me, or at least calls me when they're not standing in front of me."

She nodded. "I do, although I must admit to wanting

23

to know how you came about such a name. Are you a scoundrel?"

He did chuckle then, a low and gravelly sound that made the hairs on the back of her neck rise. "I can be when it suits. Have you always been so inquisitive?"

Willow laughed, covering her mouth with one gloved hand when those about them noticed their conversation. "Yes, I suppose. I've always been active in my friend's lives, and I like to learn new things. I do not know much about you, but you're an interesting character that I'd like to know more about."

He shook his head, staring at her. "You don't want to know about me, Miss Perry. You'll only be disappointed if you do."

"I'll be the judge of that." Willow adjusted her mask, watching the couples on the dancefloor. "Thank you for coming to my masquerade. I'm sure your presence will make my ball the talk of the town for a few days, at least."

"And you wished to be the talk about town? There are other ways to do that, without the expense of a ball."

Willow supposed that was true enough, but a ball was always preferable to nothing at all. "Yes, I suppose, but where is the fun in that, my lord?"

He threw her a wicked grin, and Willow had the impression he was talking about something else entirely than what she was speaking of. She thought over their conversation and couldn't see anything untoward or leading by it—strange man.

"Perhaps you are right, Miss Perry. A ball is much more suited to your character, and the fun I speak of is not. We are different beasts, on very different paths. I will ensure my conversation remains intellectual."

A footman passed, and Willow procured a glass of

champagne. She drank deeply, suddenly needing the sustenance. Lord Ryley was unlike any gentleman she had ever met. That he was friends with Whitstone and Duncannon did give him respectability, in her eyes at least, but still, he was an enigma to her, a man whom she could not figure out.

His short, elusive answers that were more like riddles did not help either.

"Please feel free to mingle, my lord. My friends will return soon from their dance. I do not wish to keep you if you have acquaintances here."

He didn't look at her, simply stared ahead into the crowd of guests. "I promised the duke that I would stay by you this evening. Keep you safe from gentlemen who may wish to force you into marriage by ruining your reputation. I will escort you to the retirement room should you need to go, or if you wish to stroll outside, but for tonight, my dear, you'll have to put up with my invigorating company."

Willow shut her mouth with a snap when she became conscious that she was gaping at him over his declaration. He was cosseting her like a child!

She glanced out to the ballroom floor and caught the duke and Viscount Duncannon sporadically glancing in their direction, keeping tabs while they danced. Those infuriating, maddening men! They would not get away with this.

"I do not need a man to take care of me, Lord Ryley. You may continue on elsewhere to enjoy the ball."

"Ah, you're angry. Let me assure you, Miss Perry, that it is because you're hosting a masquerade that your friends have decided that you need an escort. I have nowhere else to go in any case. No one present draws my attention. I would sooner be back at my club than scuffing the floorboards here, I assure you. But when friends ask for help, you step up and assist in any way you can."

The society tumult that happened every year when the Season commenced was a social whirlwind that some found impossible to stomach. Even Willow had felt the same a time or two when escorting her aunt about town. The sly, pitying—and some disdainful—gazes that the set her aunt had circulated with were forever etched on her mind.

Even so, hosting balls and parties, being present in the *ton*, was required if she were to marry and find true love like her friends. Granted, she may be more susceptible to fiends who would try and ruin her, but it was highly unlikely to occur. Not at events such as this.

She glanced up at his lordship, watching as he sipped his wine. His Spanish blood was prevalent in his heritage, and her fingers itched to run through his thick, dark locks. Locks that were disheveled as if he'd just rolled out of bed. His eyelashes were as opaque as a moonless night, but it was his lips that held her attention. They were full and looked as soft as hers. She studied him a moment, wondering what he would look like if he smiled, and not simply out of politeness, but out of happiness, of finding something funny that amused him.

Did he smile when at his club? If she were to visit his establishment, she could see for herself. If she found him as complicated as he was here, at least she'd know the truth of him in that small way at least.

"Just because people are wearing masks doesn't mean that I'm in any danger. Am I not standing next to the Spanish Scoundrel? Some would say that my friends have placed me directly in danger with you as my protector."

He coughed, looking at her sharply. "Afraid I'll pull you

behind a door somewhere, Miss Perry, and take your virginity? You are a virgin, are you not?" He took a sip of his wine, all nonchalance. "I've never deflowered a woman before, but I could make an exception with you. You are lovely," he said, lifting her chin with his finger and staring at her longer than what was appropriate.

Willow gasped, pulling her face free of his hold. The scoundrel! Had he really just said that? "Thank you, but I think I shall relinquish the offer. I'm going to marry a gentleman for love. A marriage similar to what my friends have been blessed with." Not a union built on lust. An emotion she felt in spades the longer she stood beside Lord Ryley. He was too magnetic. Without words or touch, he could pull a woman to his side, all the while keeping himself distant and untouchable.

"Love is all very well for some, but not suitable for everyone, I find." He glanced at their friends who were finishing up their waltz.

"I know what you're doing, my lord, and it won't work. Not with me."

"Really?" he said, grinning and giving her a little sample of his hidden charm. "What am I doing?"

"Trying to scandalize me, but while I may be shocked at the words that you use, I've not been sheltered my entire life. I went to school abroad and have friends who are of independent thought and highly opinionated. We talk about everything, men like you no exception." After meeting Lord Ryley, she wanted to know even more, if only to cure her of her interest in him. He was certainly different from the other gentlemen of her acquaintance.

"Give me time," he said, throwing her a look that made her toes want to curl up in her silk slippers.

She wouldn't let him get in the last word. "You have

the Season," she taunted, spotting Evie and leaving him where he stood. The skin on her neck prickled, and she smiled, knowing he was watching her walk away.

~

A be drank down the last of his wine as he watched Miss Willow Perry flounce off. Her sweet, intoxicating scent of jasmine teased his senses, and he wanted to chase after her skirts and continue the amusing, if not highly inappropriate, conversation they were having.

She certainly was different, perhaps even innocent in what he planned for her. Still, if she were all that was left of the Viscountess Vance's family, then Miss Willow Perry would suffer the consequences for her aunt's atrocious behavior toward his mother.

He would ruin her, he decided. Financially perhaps with her newly inherited fortune. And mayhap her reputation too. Seduce her into thinking he was her future, and then rip it away like his security was ripped away from him as a boy.

No gentleman would want her if they knew she'd been plucked. After he'd fucked her each way and sundry, she'd never look for anyone else, and the gentlemen of the *ton* would not look at her either. It was an act of delicious revenge since Miss Perry's aunt had spread the rumors about his mother regarding her loose morals with the gentlemen of their set.

All lies he'd waited years to gain retribution for.

He watched Miss Perry walk out onto the dance floor with a masked gentleman. His eyes narrowed on the man, trying to garner who it was. Without thought, his gaze traveled down Miss Perry's gown of black and red silk. She was dressed as Boudica, and he could imagine what delectable flesh lay beneath the gown. For her common blood, she was a fine specimen of feminine beauty. Her golden locks, coiffured up high on her head, brought out her large, blue eyes, her lips pouty and of the softest pink. Abe inwardly groaned, wondering if her nipples were the same light shade.

"You told her, didn't you?" Whitstone said, coming to stand beside him, looking out toward Miss Perry.

"You knew I would, and as expected, she is not at all impressed with you or Duncannon. I should expect a set down from her viperish tongue at some point. She certainly is very stubborn." Abe watched as Miss Perry's dance partner pulled her close during a spin during the waltz. He clamped his jaw shut, reminding himself that he was to keep an eye on her, nothing more. He certainly did not want any rumors circulating about town that Marquess Ryley was showing a marked interest toward a woman that he had every intention of ruining.

His blood pumped fast through his veins at the thought of seeing the only living relative of Viscountess Vance fall on his sword. A woman he had access to through mutual friends. He grinned, taking a sip of his drink.

"What are you planning? You look like you've concocted a scheme." Whitstone came to stand before him, cutting off his view of Miss Perry. "You're not to dally with Willow unless you intend to marry her. Do not cross me on that, Ryley."

He raised his brow at Whitstone's gumption. "We're friends, and I will always have your back, but don't tell me what to do. Not with anything."

Whitstone didn't move, simply stared at Abe. Abe stared back, not giving an inch. He didn't take nicely to bullies, and even though Whitstone was his friend, he still would not tolerate being told what to do. His mother had been bullied, practically forced to scuttle back to Spain. Never would he tolerate the same treatment or influence in his life.

"She's a sweet woman and Ava's best friend. Do not play with her."

"I have no intention of playing with her," he said, only partially lying to his friend. While he may not physically play with her, not yet at least, he would play with her security. He'd lost his mother and the security of her presence at a young age. It was only fair that Viscountess Vance's niece suffered the same fate.

"Thank you," Whitstone said, clapping him on the back and guiding him toward Duncannon. "Now, come with me. Duncannon and I are looking to invest in sugar and we'd like your opinion."

"Of course." Abe let the duke guide him over to Duncannon. He sporadically watched Miss Perry as her dance partner escorted her back over to where the Duchess Whitstone and Countess Duncannon stood. She smiled and dipped into a neat curtsy to the gentleman, bidding him a thank you. Her eyes met his over the gentleman's shoulders. His gut clenched as if he'd been physically punched, and he took a deep, calming breath. What the hell was wrong with him? Too little wine he'd imagine.

The way Miss Perry looked at him told him she'd be an easy mark. She may be annoyed tonight that she'd been manhandled by her friends, but with a few sweet words, and gentlemanly behavior, he'd gain her trust. And then and only then would he take his revenge.

He must have grinned a little as a light, rosy hue spread

across her cheeks before she looked away, severing their moment.

Abe nodded to something the duke said, trying to gauge what his friends were discussing. The Season had only just commenced, and perhaps this year, to gain all that he wanted, he would have to partake a little more than usual.

Not the most terrible inconvenience to suffer. Not when at last he'd get what he'd always wanted.

Revenge.

CHAPTER 4

*W*illow sat before Ava and Hallie in the duchess's private parlor at their London townhouse and fought to keep her calm. "You had your husbands and their friend guard me the entire night of the Masquerade. What were you thinking, doing such a thing?"

Ava worked her hands in her lap, her face ashen. She should be ashamed. Never would Willow ever think to do such a thing to either of them. "I'm sorry, Willow. We were only thinking of your best interest."

"Really?" Willow said, raising her brow. "When you came to London before you married the duke... Did I follow you home when you left one particular ball only to find out later that you met with the duke in my aunt's parlor? I never chastised you over your actions that night now, did I?"

At her friend's silence, Willow turned to Hallie. "Nor did I impose on you every day at your dig site in Somerset to ensure you were always well-chaperoned. Which, if you remember, I should have since you had intimate relations with the viscount in a tent."

Hallie giggled and slapped her hand over her face. Willow glared at her friends. They were impossible! "Going forward, I think we can safely say that you will stop mollycoddling me as if I'm a child. We're almost the same age. I have a chaperone and two companions. Tell your husbands, the dears that they are, that they need to walk away and leave me to enjoy the little freedom I have before I marry."

"You're engaged?" Ava asked, sitting forward on her chair.

"Who to?" Hallie blurted a second later.

Willow sat back in her chair, sipping her sweet tea. "Oh, I'm not betrothed just yet, but I'm sure that will happen this Season. I know I'm unable to live as I am forever. Society would eventually shun me for such insolence, and I do wish for a family, and so the prospect is agreeable. But to meet a man that makes my heart beat fast, my skin to prickle, I must be left alone to have the opportunity to speak to him." The image of Lord Ryley flittered through her mind. He'd made her heart thump so loud in her chest she thought he might hear, and as for her senses, each time he touched her, it was as if a million little pins pricked her flesh, making the fine hairs stand on end.

Not that she would look at him as a possible husband. He was rude, abrupt, authoritative, and there was something about him that was raw, unkempt. Animal-like. A wolf perhaps. Unpredictable, and one never knew if it would bite or lick you.

Heat rushed up her neck at the idea of Lord Ryley licking her. Oh, dear lord, she needed to stop thinking of him.

"And Lord Ryley, Willow?" Evie queried. "Did you wish for Ava and Hallie to have his attendance on you cease?"

"I do, yes. I shall leave that in the hands of you fine ladies. And now there is something else I wish to ask you all."

"What is it?" Molly sat herself down on the settee between Ava and Hallie, her cheeks pink from standing in front of the window these past minutes. London was warm today, and Willow had planned on going for a ride in Hyde Park this afternoon. Not that it was the social hour, but she didn't care about that. She merely wanted Rotten Row all to herself.

Willow caught everyone's attention, needing to ensure they were all listening. "I want to do something a little scandalous, and I want you all to do it with me."

Hallie chuckled, sitting forward. "Do tell us what you want."

Evie nodded vigorously.

"You know as well as anyone that I've led a mundane life under the care of my aunt. And while I'll be ever thankful for all that she did for me and for leaving me her estate, I want to live. I want to sneak into balls we've not been invited to. I want to spend a night at Covent Gardens, and lastly, I want to visit Hell's Gate. Why should it be only the men who experience these places?"

"I think you're under an illusion if you think only men visit Hell's Gate," Ava interjected.

Molly gasped. "Are you saying there are women of the *demimonde* that frequent there?"

Ava chuckled. "And more."

"Has the duke ever been?" Willow asked, unsure what she thought of her friend's husbands spending nights in such a lewd and dissolute place. Not that it made her any less curious as to what went on within its walls, but she wasn't the one married here. A little voice reminded her she was female, however…

"He's not been since we married, but I do believe he used to visit quite often. Whitstone was frequently the talk of London if you remember."

Willow remembered well having spent some seasons in London with the duke before he earned back the love of her friend. "I want to visit there. We'll wear masks or dress like men, but I think it would be fun."

Hallie threw her a consoling smile. "While I would love to see the inside of Hell's Gate, I better not be caught there. I will, however, accompany you to parties and balls we're not invited to and Covent Garden. I see no harm in that."

"I agree with Hallie," Ava said.

Willow looked to Evie and Molly, both of who were wide-eyed and quiet. "Well, are you in or out, you two?"

"I'm in," Evie said, smiling. "I'm definitely in."

"I think I'd prefer to read a book at home if you do not mind," Molly stated.

While Willow did hope for all her friends to come with her, she could understand their choices. "Very well, each of us must make her choice." She turned to Evie. "It looks like it's just going to be us two."

Evie stood, bouncing a little on the spot. "This is going to be so much fun. I can hardly wait to see what the men of our acquaintance get up to while in London."

"I should say quite a lot," Ava interjected. "You must ensure that however you dress, you're unable to be identified. Maybe a gentleman with his mistress may be less obvious, a disguise such as that."

"That would certainly work." Hallie reached for the teapot, pouring herself another cup. "I'm sure Viscountess Vance has some old wigs that you could cut down into a man's design."

"You're taller than me, Willow. It's probably best that you dress as a man," Evie said with a decided nod.

All true, but the thought of being dressed in breeches, to be so exposed, did make her question her choice. Could she do this?

"Breeches are liberating, Willow. You'll enjoy wearing them." Hallie sipped her tea, grinning.

Exhilaration drummed through her veins at the thought of being so scandalous and secretive. She'd never once stepped out of the proper shell her aunt had encased her in. That could all change now. So long as she didn't get caught, behaved herself, her night at Hell's Gate would end perfectly well. Dressed as a man, no one would recognize her, and Evie with a mask would be even less recognizable. Her friend had been languishing in the country, so the *ton* hardly knew who she was. It was a perfect plan.

"When should we do it?" Evie asked, her eyes bright with expectation.

"Tomorrow? I think I can have my maid be ready by then." Willow chuckled and picking up her teacup, took a sip, cataloging everything she needed to prepare before their night out in London.

A side of London they'd never seen before and would never see again. One night would be enough, and she'd been happy with that.

"Sounds perfect," Evie said.

"Sounds absurd," Molly retorted, shaking her head.

Willow grinned at Evie. "You ready to play my doxie, Evie dear?"

"Oh yes. I most certainly am."

≈

*T*he following evening Willow sat in the hackney cab they had hired for the evening, adjusting her cravat, and checking again the buttons on her breeches were indeed fastened.

"You look so handsome," Evie said, "a perfect lover for me."

Willow took in her friend's red, silk gown with a bodice that was so low that her breasts threatened to spill from her gown. Her little black hat and netting overlay disguised her face enough that no one should be able to recognize her. The blonde wig also helped, covering her dark locks.

As for Willow, her hair was braided under a man's wig. Her maid had been able to fashion it out of one of her aunt's old wigs. With a little makeup, they had attempted to make her skin about her jaw represent a shadow as if she were unshaven. Her breasts were wrapped tight behind a linen bandage. It was probably the most uncomfortable thing about her disguise. Her breasts weren't small, and to be so tightly wound wasn't natural.

"Are we going to gamble? I brought some pin money just in case."

"I think we must if we're not to look suspicious. Feel free to drape yourself over me during any games we partake. We must act the part."

Evie sighed. "I've always wanted to act. Of course, it's not open for women such as us, but even so, I do love the stage. We should spend a night at the theater. I know it's not a scandalous pastime, but we do not attend often enough."

"We will, I promise. Maybe later this week?" Willow offered, wanting to give her friends anything that they asked, especially after Evie was so kind as to come with her tonight and put her reputation on the line.

The carriage rocked to a halt, and the door opened. A man dressed in black breeches and a superfine coat reached into the carriage to assist them. Evie took the man's hand, and Willow reminded herself that he'd not slighted her by letting her alight herself. With her dressed as a man, the servant would not be expected to help her down. She took Evie's arm, slipping it around hers, and started toward the doors to Lord Ryley's club.

The muffled sound of music sounded from behind the wooden door, and another servant opened it, bowing to them as they passed.

Willow swallowed her gasp at the sight of the club. It was situated in what looked to be an old warehouse, industrial and cold. Yet, the chandeliers, the yards of colored silk drapes that hung from the ceiling across the room, giving secretive nooks that those who wanted privacy could slip away into made the room decadent and wicked.

A gray smoke haze floated near the roof, the deep timbre of men's conversation, and the tinkling sound of the women's laughter met Willow's ears. She stepped forward, giving Evie's hand a comforting pat as her friend stiffened at her side.

"Men are looking at me."

Willow narrowed her eyes, taking in those who would gawp at her lady friend. Many men were salivating at the sight of Evie. A shiver of unease slipped down her spine that perhaps this was a bad idea.

"Don't show any reaction to them. Lift your chin and

stare them down. They'll soon realize you're not interested."

Willow spotted a staircase that led up to a second level. Glancing up, she spied a row of doors. Rooms perhaps where couples could become entirely familiarized with each other. They walked farther into the room, and Willow spotted a table free for *vingt-et-un*. She sat down, pulling out some notes from her pocket and bid the dealer to commence. Others joined in on the game, and twice she won a round against the dealer before losing all she'd accumulated by breaking over twenty-one.

Evie leaned over her shoulder. "Lord Ryley is watching us."

Willow stilled, her stomach roiling as if she were on a runaway horse. She glanced up and locked eyes with the very man that vexed her to no end. He was glaring at her, and a muscle in his jaw flexed as he continued to watch them.

She placed another bet on the table, ignoring the fact that her skin burned with his notice. "Do not look at him. He'll think we're hiding something."

Out of her peripheral sight, she noticed he moved farther into the room, and she chanced a glance and couldn't see him anymore. Willow sighed in relief, having thought he'd recognized her.

"Sir, I do not believe we've been introduced."

The deep, gravelly voice sounded behind her, and Evie gasped, standing upright. "Oh, hello, my lord. Ye do look very handsome tonight, I must say."

Willow glanced at Evie as her voice took on the familiar twang of an East London whore. She pushed down her fear and remembered to lower her tone. "We have not." She turned back to the game, gesturing for the dealer to start another round, ignoring Lord Ryley. Her mind raced for a name to come up with and...nothing. Nothing would come to mind.

Blast it all to hell.

Silence ensued, before his tall, muscular form slumped into a chair beside her. He laid money on the table. "You're new in town. Your name was?"

He frowned at her, waiting for a reply, and she swallowed. Why hadn't she thought of a blasted surname? "Frank Marsh at your service, my lord. Simply visiting town and wanting to enjoy a night out with my girl."

Evie tittered beside her, but Willow could feel Lord Ryley's inspection of her like a caress, slipping over her skin and leaving her breathless in its wake.

Lord Ryley nodded, a contemplative look on his face, before he leaned in close, catching her eye. "You will finish this game, Miss Perry, and then you will come to my office. It's the last door on your left when you make the second-floor landing. Your whore," he said, his gaze flicking to Evie. "Can wait with mine." He gestured toward a woman who stood to the side of the room, her black gown transparent and showing all her assets to anyone who looked. Heat bloomed on Willow's cheeks, and she fought not to gasp. "Evie will be safe with Lottie while we complete our little chat."

He pushed back his chair, leaving her gaping at his retreating back. Her gaze slid down his spine to land on his breeches. A perfectly shaped derriere that one could ogle to their heart's content.

"He's going to kill us," Evie squeaked, gasping as Lottie came over to them, smiling at Evie. Willow was taken aback by the woman's beauty, and a pang of jealousy spiked through her that this woman shared Lord Ryley's bed. Knew him intimately. Had his delectable, sinful lips on hers.

"This way, if you please. We have a retiring room you may use, miss."

Willow pushed back her chair and waited to ensure Evie was safe with Lottie before she turned and started in the direction Lord Ryley had gone. The gambling hell was full now. People jostled as she walked toward the staircase, women groaned and laughed as men made use of their assets.

Willow kept her eyes forward, her face a mask of indifference. The thought that she looked feminine and that had been why Lord Ryley had recognized her would not abate. Did everyone who cast glances upon her and Evie recognize them? His lordship certainly had.

She stepped onto the bottom step of the staircase, pausing. What did his lordship want to say to her? Was he going to scold her, scream and shout? She'd not put up with such treatment if he did. This club did allow women, and she was in disguise, even if not the most foolproof one it would seem. Even so, he could throw them out on their ears.

Willow glanced about, torn over her decision to run like the devil himself was after her, or confront him. Either one was not a welcoming thought.

~

*A*be paced in his office, stopping now and then to take a calming breath. Damn Miss Willow Perry to Hades and back. He'd not thought to see her again after his coddling of her at the masquerade ball the other evening. He'd made a conscious decision that he would not

41

attend any more events with Miss Perry present. He could financially ruin her without having to see the chit. It was easy enough to have someone infiltrate whoever looked after her money, place it into high-risk investments that never had a hope of earning a profit.

He'd placed his man of business on doing that very thing only yesterday, so to see her today, bright-eyed and delectably dressed in breeches of all things was not what he'd wanted to see. Coward, perhaps he was, but to take a woman down was easier to do when one did not have to look her in the eye.

He checked his pocket watch. She'd been longer than five minutes. Where was she?

He wrenched his office door open, stepping out onto the balcony hallway and watched as Miss Perry and her friend all but ran toward the door. For a moment, he allowed himself to watch the perfect sway of her ass as she hightailed it out of the club. The idea of not having a private audience with her irked, and he leaned on the railing, contemplating going after her or chasing her down at the next social event she would attend.

She needed to know that to come here, she risked her reputation. After he was finished with her, there would be little to recommend her to any gentleman searching for a wife. She ought to take more care with her behavior.

His manservant and guard at the door opened it for the parting guests, and at the very last minute, Miss Perry turned and looked directly at him. His gut clenched at the challenging, haughty look she bestowed on him, and he smirked.

Taking down Miss Willow Perry would be a victory worth savoring. What a pity that he couldn't savor his victory between her legs.

CHAPTER 5

Their night out was a disaster. Willow stared at her reflection before her dressing table mirror, her eyes wide and bright, her male wig a little crooked, wisps of long, blonde locks slipped across her brow. Her cheeks were as pink as Evie's gown, and she couldn't have looked more feminine if she tried. She cringed. Any wonder Lord Ryley had recognized her. Studying herself now, she wondered how she had ever thought she could pull off this farce in the first place—an absurd notion.

Which begged the question, who else spied her and knew who she was? Some would call her foolish for partaking in such a venture, and they would be right.

Willow pulled the wig from her head, running her fingers over her scalp before she started to undo the braids. The feel of being free from the wig's restraint was delightful, and she sighed as she massaged her hair loose. She undressed quickly, slipping on a silk chemise, one of her indulgences since her aunt's passing, before climbing into bed.

Willow stared up at the darkened roof, the crackle of the fire the only sound in the room. Her body felt tight and fidgety, and she rolled onto her side, attempting to find a comfortable position. The image of Lord Ryley glancing at her, his dark, hooded eyes that followed her every move would not leave her. Worse was the fact that somewhere deep inside, she liked having him watch her.

At the masquerade ball, his words that he was present to keep her safe from harm had sent a frisson of desire to shoot to her core. He was a handsome man, powerful and well-connected, and as sinful as the devil himself.

He certainly looked like the dark lord when he leaned over the railing at his club when she fled, his lips twisting into an amused grin.

Willow sighed, rolling onto her back, thumping the bedding at her side. If only she had a husband, she'd not be so fixated on a man whom she'd promised herself to dismiss as a likely candidate as a husband. There was little doubt he thought highly of himself and very little of others whom he deemed unsuitable as friends. That he thought women should be protected, swaddled in cotton, was not a becoming trait for a man. Not for a woman like Willow in any case. She enjoyed her independence and had learned long ago how to look after herself. Losing her parents young had achieved that and then being sent away to school in France.

Even so, the idea of Lord Ryley crawling up over the bed to lay atop her, bestowing kiss after delicious kiss on her exposed skin, sent an exquisite bolt of need to her core. He was a tall man, broad shoulders, and with muscular thighs. No doubt his many years owning a bawdy club had ensured he was athletic and fit. His height would typically suit her, being a tall meg herself. What a pity he was determined to remain scandalous and nothing else.

Willow slid her hand over her stomach, closing her eyes as her fingers speared through the thatch of curls at the apex of her thighs. She rubbed her fingers against her skin, having read that for a woman to find pleasure, this is where they should touch.

As always, she found the caress to be pointless. It did hint of something more, made her feel tingly and relaxed, but never anything exploding or mind-numbing happened as she'd heard women whisper throughout her many Seasons.

Tonight was no different. Willow bit her lip, thinking of Lord Ryley's large hands, imagining them over her breasts, squeezing her nipples. She rolled her nipples between her thumbs and forefingers, gasping as the action shot a bolt of pleasure to her core.

Her interest piqued. Now, that was different. She'd never reacted to her touch in such a way before. The thought of Lord Ryley touching her, teasing and kissing her made her body hum with need.

And yet, after a time, nothing happened that was overly exciting. What was she doing wrong?

Willow groaned, rolling over once more, pulling the blankets up beneath her neck. There was no use. She would have to wait until she had a husband to find out what all the fuss was about. The image of Lord Ryley flashed through her mind, and she squeezed her legs together, wondering what a night with him would be like. A night in his arms so he could show her all that could be between a husband and wife.

"It would be delicious," she said to herself, knowing she'd never said a more accurate statement. The Spanish

Scoundrel would be as wicked in a bed as he was in person. That she had little doubt.

~

Two days later, after a summons from the Duchess of Whitstone, Willow was seated into a highly sprung carriage, luggage piled atop the vehicle, headed into the country. Evie and Molly sat across from her, chatting about their little sojourn to Hampton.

"Ava seemed very excited about the new estate. Do you know much about it?" Evie asked, looking out the window and taking in the passing streets of London.

"Only that the duke purchased it for her so they could be closer to London and also have the ability to train horses during the Season. You know how much Ava loves her horses."

"And so this is a house party? Or is it a small group of friends only that will be there?" Molly asked.

"I believe the duke will have some guests, but I understand it's only us that Ava has invited, and Hallie, of course."

Willow glanced down at her folded hands in her lap, refusing to give way to the hope that one particular friend of the duke's would be present. A silly notion. The man was busy, what with his infamous club, and no doubt numerous lovers to keep satisfied, so she doubted Lord Ryley would be present.

Still, her nights continued with images of him, of his dark, hooded gaze sliding over her, dipping to her lips whenever he spoke. Did he imagine kissing her as she imagined kissing him? Willow bit her lip, knowing she'd thought of little else but what it would feel like to be in his arms. A consummate lover who knew how to play a woman as well as any musician playing his instrument.

In under two hours, they were pulling up before the "cottage" as Ava had described her new home. Willow stepped out of the carriage, untying her bonnet as she took in the magnificent estate. The front door opened, and Ava stepped outside, waving.

"You're here. I'm so glad you could come." Their friend greeted them, hugging each in turn before ushering them into the house. "Come inside. We're about to have luncheon."

Willow couldn't believe the size of the house. It was as big as the duchess's main estate in Berkshire. "Ava, this is not a cottage." They entered the foyer, a large, marble staircase leading upstairs. Two footmen came to take their hats and gloves, and Willow handed them off, unable to take her observation off the home.

"It's lovely, isn't it? My darling husband spoils me."

"What does your darling husband do?" the duke asked, coming to stand beside Ava and wrapping his arm about her waist.

Evie chuckled at the duke's and duchess's public display of affection. Willow smiled at the genuine love that radiated off them.

"Only what is expected of him, my dear," Ava said, a teasing glint in her eye.

The sound of footsteps behind the duke caught Willow's attention, and she glanced over his shoulder. Her heart jumped into her throat at the sight of who strolled casually toward them. Lord Ryley took each of them in before his wicked gaze landed on her and stilled.

He bowed, all proper manners. Willow remembered to dip into a curtsy.

"Ladies, it's lovely to see you again," Lord Ryley said, watching Willow.

She raised her chin. He would not intimidate her, nor would she allow him to chastise her over being caught at his club. It wasn't a private locale. She could attend if she wished. No one other than his lordship knew she'd seen his gambling den in any case, so what did it matter?

Willow heard Molly and Evie mumble a reply, but she did not. Instead, she turned back to the duke and duchess. "After lunch, will you take us on a tour of the home and grounds? I understand you have horses here already."

"We do," Ava said, clearly excited to have some of her hairy children so close. "Would you care for a ride this afternoon?"

"I would love one," Willow said without thought. She loved to ride, and although she wasn't as good as Ava, she was the only other friend in their set who could keep up with the duchess. With Hallie expecting with Viscount Duncannon, she would not join in, and Evie and Molly rarely rode at all.

"Come," the duke said, turning toward a room off to the side of the foyer. "We were about to have lunch and would like you to join us, unless you would prefer to freshen up first."

"Lunch will be welcome," Willow replied, looking to Evie and Molly for their approval. They nodded, and so they started toward the dining room. Lord Ryley hung back, allowed the duke and duchess to pass, along with their friends, but stepped in front of Willow when she went to follow.

"Hello, Miss Perry. Or should I ask you what particular name you'll be using this week while here in Hampton?"

"Willow will do well enough, my lord." She slipped

past him, and he came into step beside her. "Did you enjoy your evening out the other night?"

The tips of her ears burned, and she feigned ignorance. "I do not know what you're talking about, my lord." His deep, evocative chuckle did odd things to her stomach, pulsed heat to her core. The man was a walking scandal, and he knew it.

"Come now. Your secret is safe with me. I was, however, disappointed you did not come to my office to discuss the matter. To enlighten me."

She gasped, meeting his eyes. Was he flirting with her? Or was she reading into his words more than she ought because she wanted him to flirt with her? Wanting him to touch her as the duke touched Ava. For so many years, she'd been the perfect companion, never stepping out of line or saying the wrong thing. Scandalous of her, but she was tired of always being proper. She wanted to live, explore, love, find a husband who joined her on life's journey. Have children and see the world.

"I can always revisit you, my lord." She grinned at him, and his eyes widened. A chuckle escaped her at his shock, and she was glad she was able to turn the tables against him. It was highly unlikely that he was ever on the receiving end of such banter, not from a woman of her status, at least. His dashing Cyprians perhaps like to tease, but virginal women who were once companions did not.

He reached out and pulled her to a stop before the door. Willow watched as the others prepared to sit, before turning a raised brow at his lordship. "Is something the matter, my lord?" she asked, her tone sweet and innocent, even though she knew her retort discombobulated him.

"You're never to return to Hell's Gate, Miss Perry. Ever.

It's not a place for a lady of your constitution, and it's not safe for you to be in that part of town."

She patted his arm condescendingly. "Now, now, my lord. Don't make us be at odds with each other. Not when I was starting to like you a little. You have kept my presence at your club a secret from your friends, after all. Do not ruin it by telling me what I can and cannot do."

A muscle ticked in his jaw as his dark, consuming gaze stared down at her. If he were trying to scare her into submission, he would fail. There was nothing more she liked than a challenge, and although she'd never had one of the male variety before, there was always a first.

His gaze dipped to her lips, and without thought, she dampened them with her tongue. His nose flared, his jaw clenched, and fire simmered in her blood. He was attracted to her. No matter what he may say to the contrary, his reactions to her were telling.

Interesting…

"Should I tell our friends you were at Hell's Gate?" His deep voice held a warning any sane woman would heed. She was not one of them.

"A better question is, will you tell them? I can always counteract your words by telling the duke and viscount that you invited me into your office instead of bundling me into a carriage. One does wonder why you did that." She grinned, leaning close. "I hope you weren't thinking of dallying with me, that would never do."

Although after the last few nights that were consumed with images of him above her, touching and kissing her, a dalliance may be preferable.

"If I wanted to trifle with you, what makes you think I need an office, Miss Perry?" He pushed past her and went to seat himself at the dining room table.

She stared after him, the thought of such a thing making her skin shiver. Was it even possible? Were couples doing such a thing in public, and she'd never noticed? Extraordinary.

Willow sat herself to the side of Whitstone. She laid the linen napkin over her lap, taking in the place settings, and seeing who was present. The duke and duchess sat at the heads of the table, Lord Ryley, directly across from her. He caught her eye as he sipped his wine, and she read the challenge in his deep-brown orbs that looked almost black under the candlelight. Sin camouflaged as a gentleman in a superfine coat.

"I understand Ava is taking you riding this afternoon. We've brought down some hacks for everyone to use, so you'll be quite safe."

She turned, smiling at the duke whom she loved as much as a brother, if she'd had one. "Thank you. Ava's been kind enough recently to help me in purchasing a horse of my own. I've always loved riding, but as you know, my aunt didn't like me too far away from her at any one moment."

"I remember."

The first course of soup was served, and the delicious scent of vegetables wafted up and made her stomach clench, reminding her that she'd not eaten this morning. They ate in relative silence for a time, the small hum of conversation around the table sporadic, the subject matter what the guests intended to do over the next week at the house party.

"This is a wonderful idea having a home so close to London. And one that has acreage. I should imagine you'll have Ava with you more often now, Your Grace."

He smiled across at his wife, and she smiled back. A

pang of longing shot through Willow. She wanted a love like that. All-consuming and grand. One of those loves that people like Lord Byron wrote poems about.

As if drawn, her gaze slid to Lord Ryley seated beside Hallie, Countess Duncannon. He was undoubtedly the type of man that love sonnets were composed for, all those long, dark eyelashes that were prettier than her own, his skin a golden hue that made hers look washed out and pasty. He was everything a woman dreamed about, trouble that would be hard to rid oneself of.

He was certainly not marriageable material. Too many scandals, too many lovers to contend with, and men like Lord Ryley would never be content to lay with one woman for the rest of his life. No. He would like his cake and to eat it as well.

Ava caught his attention, and he turned to her friend, his face changing to one of interest and pleasure at having Hallie by his side. How changeable men could be when they needed to be.

"Are you settling into your new home and way of life, Willow? If you ever need any financial advice you know you can come to Duncannon or me. Our doors are always open."

"Thank you, that is very kind. I do wish to look at investments in the next few months. The law firm which handles my interests believes it may be a way to grow my income. I haven't had time to look into it as yet. After the Season perhaps I will."

"Lord Ryley has multiple investments, both commercial and financial. You should seek him out while you're both here in Hampton, see what he suggests. I know he would never lead you astray."

To do such a thing would mean she would have to

solicit his help. Not an entirely awful idea, which in itself was problematic. As much as she may long for his hands on her, for his kisses and whatever else he could show her, such a path would only lead to ruin and disappointment. To give herself to such a man would mean risking her heart, and she had that saved up for a gentleman who would be willing to give his in return. Lord Ryley was not one of them.

"Would you ask him for me, Your Grace? We're not the best of friends I'm afraid, and I would find it uncomfortable asking his lordship for financial advice."

The duke frowned, turning to her. "Has he offended you in any way?"

His grace glared at Lord Ryley, and she touched his arm, bringing his attention back to her. "No. No, Your Grace. Nothing like that, but I fear we're just destined never to be friends, and that is all very well." She glanced at Lord Ryley, heat pooling in her belly at his smile toward Hallie when she spoke. "I have the impression that he disapproves of me for some reason. As if I've done something that has offended him."

"You must be mistaken, Willow, but I shall talk to him on your behalf and ensure all is well and that he is compliant in helping you in your investments. I have full faith that he will take care of you and not lead you astray."

She nodded, smiling at the duke, not wanting him to know that the thought of Lord Ryley leading her amiss left her breathless and warm. "Thank you, Your Grace. You two are too kind to me."

"No, we're not. We're friends, and that's what friends do."

The remainder of lunch was pleasant, and talk of her impending ride let her forget her troubles with the brooding marquess across from her. At least out on the estate with Ava, she would not have to deal with him this afternoon. One consolation she supposed even though the idea of not sparring with him left her more dejected than discharged.

CHAPTER 6

*H*e was in hell. Literally. He rode behind the duchess, and Miss Perry, who in a trot rose and fell on her seat, her delectable rump all too visible to him in his current position. She wore a deep-navy riding gown, but instead of wearing a skirt and riding astride, she had donned a pair of matching navy breeches and was riding astride like the duchess.

Abe inwardly groaned. There was something wrong with him to be mooning over the chit whom he wanted to bring down, to topple from her lofty level that her aunt had placed her upon. Not fair, he knew, to make a relative pay for the sins of someone else, but it was his only recourse. The Vance family would fall. Their treatment of his mother had ensured she fell from grace. Miss Perry was part of the rotting London society he steered clear of. She was the only living blood relative of Viscountess Vance, and therefore she would fall.

That did not mean that he could not play with the chit for a little while before he brought her low. He had been going to stay well away from her, keep her at a distance.

Much easier not to know your prey, but there was something about Miss Perry that drew him in—aggravated and enticed.

The duchess and Miss Perry stopped under the shade of a tree to rest, and he joined them. His attention snapped to her long legs. They would fit about his waist perfectly.

He shut his eyes, dismissing the visual of them tangled in bed, sheets askew, her hair mussed from his attentions, her cheeks pinkened from release. Her mouth open on a gasp before he covered it with his.

God damn it.

He should go into the village tonight and find some release for his aching balls. He could not continue thinking of Miss Perry in such a way. In any way. She was his nemesis. The woman he would destroy. She was not the woman that stirred his loins. He wouldn't allow it.

Liar, a voice whispered in his ear.

"I'm going to go for a gallop. Did you want to join me?" Ava asked, glancing over the land.

"Not today, Ava. I'm not quite ready for that as yet," Miss Perry said.

"I will keep Miss Perry company, Your Grace. Feel free to go for your ride."

The duchess nodded to him, and then turned her mount, pushing it into a blistering pace. He adjusted his seat, his cock aching with his imaginings of them alone. A quiet settled between them, only the sound of birds in the trees and the slight rustling of wind through the grasses impinging on their solitude.

Abe studied her profile as she glanced in the direction the duchess had ridden, in no way inclined to speak to him it would seem. Her ignoring of him irked and he cleared his throat.

"You ride well, better than I thought you would."

"I've always liked to ride, but don't get enough time to do so. I'll be changing that now that I'm on my own."

He narrowed his eyes, disliking the idea of her being by herself. Her house on Hanover Square was one of the largest in London, and she was a woman after all. Anyone could take advantage of her.

Abe ran a hand through his hair, knowing he was hell-bent on being that person who took advantage of her. The one to bring her down to the level the Vances should be. He couldn't start to let his emotions get involved in his plan. Yes, Miss Perry was spirited, intelligent, and beautiful, but she was also a Vance. Hailed from a bloodline that was as vicious as a snake.

"I did not expect to see you here at the duke and duchess's estate. I wouldn't think that such an outing would be wild enough for you, my lord."

He clamped his jaw against a cutting retort that his life was so excessive, that he could not enjoy the slower parts of it. Such as they were now, out on a horse in the middle of the countryside. "I do not always live in London. I do have two country estates that I attend several times a year. I think you must believe me to be very idle indeed."

She shrugged, and the action brought his attention to her bodice. The tight, navy-blue spencer that sat over her riding attire, accentuating her breasts. He swallowed, his gaze traveling over her person. After the other evening, when he'd seen her dressed as a man, he'd thought that perhaps he'd been mistaken as to the size of her breasts, but he was not. They were full and lush and rose with every breath. A lovely handful. A wicked mouthful.

"I will not lie and say I have wondered how you fill

your day, but I could not imagine the answer and so gave up on the notion."

He chuckled and stilled at the realization that he'd not laughed in a very long time. And yet, here he was, sitting under an Oak tree with the woman he was determined to ruin, and she'd made him laugh.

She glanced at him, her eyes widening. The deep blue of her gaze watching him with something akin to shock.

"I not only run my gambling club, but I also sit in on parliament, and I have numerous investments that I manage. Speaking of which, the duke has asked me to assist you. He mentioned you may be interested in investing in such schemes.

"Schemes? I do hope any investments that I partake in are more than schemes, my lord."

Again, his lips twitched. This woman would be a worthy opponent and would keep him on his toes. Her downfall would be all the sweeter for it.

"They are, I assure you, Miss Perry." He adjusted his seat, curious about her past. "You were your aunt's companion. How long did you care for her?"

She sighed, glancing up at the clouds. "Eight years or so. I've been her companion since returning from school in France. As much as I loved my aunt, and I'll be forever grateful for her kindness toward me, I cannot help but be thankful that I did not live my entire life under servitude. It is not easy being at the beck and call to others all the time. My situation was better than most, being a relative, but it was not easy."

"I should imagine not." Not that he could really imagine at all. He'd always had servants, people doing his bidding. The idea that she was one of those people who had served men and women like him left him cold.

"Because of my past employment, I've decided to allow my staff to have rostered holidays throughout the year. Everyone deserves a little time away, to restore and remember that there is more to life than just work."

Abe frowned over his horse's ears, unsure he'd ever heard something so absurd or brilliant in his life. There wasn't a day that he did not work, did not overlook, and check in on all the little particulars that made up his life. He did not have time off, so why should his staff?

Miss Perry's take on the subject was interesting and worth thinking over. To drop all commitments, to leave and go elsewhere, a place to do nothing but relax both terrified and tempted him in equal parts.

"You saw yourself as being in service? You were a viscountess's niece, I do not think you were ever at risk of making your fingers bleed from too much embroidery."

"Have you ever sat all day and embroidered, my lord?"

He met her eyes, shaking his head. "I have not," he admitted.

"Then until you have, I suggest you keep your opinions to yourself."

Abe shut his mouth with a snap. Unsure how to respond to the set down.

For a moment, they sat atop their horses, the sight of the duchess on a faraway hill the only movement about them. "I cannot make you out, my lord," she continued. "You profess to work all the time. That you are busy and important."

He clenched his jaw at the sarcasm he heard in her tone, condemned to hear her out at least before he administered one of his own set downs.

"And yet you treat me as if when I lived with my aunt, I did nothing at all. She was a very private woman, disliked anyone knowing her business, and so it was left to me to take care of her all the time. Bathing, dressing, relieving of herself in the middle of the night all fell on me. For years, not months. I attended to her at balls and parties. I ensured she always had her favorite food for supper. I went on endless calls to her friends, day in, day out. Do not speak to me as if I do not know a day's work in my life. I know it well. Better than you, I should imagine. When last did you empty the piss pot from under your bed?"

He stared at her aghast. She emptied the chamber pot. Good god, her aunt was as bad as he'd always known her to be. Abe took in the defiant rise of Miss Perry's chin, and a little of his distaste toward her shifted. Maybe she was also a victim of her aunt. Not in the way that his mother endured, but in a demoralizing way. The way one eventually accepted their fate and lost their voice to say otherwise.

"I apologize if I came across as condescending. I see that I was wrong."

She shook her head, adjusting her seat. "My aunt ensured I was educated, and I thank her every day she sent me to France to learn, or I may have never known Ava, Hallie, Evie, and Molly, but I can also thank her for showing me that the staff that rush about for us are people too. They have lives just like you and I. They too dream for a better future. I see that now, and I will never go back to the way it was during my aunt's life. My servants are happier, always going about their work with a spring in their step. I did that because I understood their plight."

"You must be commended for your forward-thinking." Abe frowned at his own words. What was he saying? Complimenting her for being radical. Even so, the idea had merit and was worth considering implementing into his own homes. If it meant that his staff was more congenial, went about their chores in a more timely and productive manner, he would test the idea forthwith.

She threw him a small smile, and his chest tightened. Damn it. He didn't need to feel sorry for the chit. That wasn't why he was here, why he jumped at the chance to help her with her investments when the duke asked. He wanted her to pay for her family's betrayal toward his. And damn it, he would make her pay. Some way or another.

"Thank you, Lord Ryley."

~

*W*illow took in the overbearing, too-handsome-for-his-own-good gentleman seated beside her on his horse and reveled in his attraction. Never had she ever had this feeling that she felt when around this man. As if her body gravitated toward him, wanted to be near his person, his sphere. A sense of rightness that went against her morals.

The lord was a rascal, a rake by town standards, and he was undoubtedly not marriageable material. He was obnoxious and rude and had little idea of how to treat his staff.

Being unmarried as she was, even at her advanced age, some would say decidedly on the shelf, he wasn't someone she could dally with. Have a scandalous, clandestine affair.

As much as he tempted her to be scandalous, she could never do it. She chewed on her bottom lip, debating that fact in her mind. Placing all the pros and cons together and seeing what that sum equaled.

"I'd love to know what you're thinking right at this moment, Miss Perry."

His deep, curious voice broke into her musings, and she

met his eyes. She grappled for some excuse as to why she was caught ogling him. "I wasn't thinking of anything. Merely pondering."

"Would you like to go for a walk? I believe there is a stream not far from here. The horses can be watered before we return."

She patted her mount, distracting her hands enough so they didn't reach out to test one of her pro theories that his lordship was a skilled kisser as she presumed him to be. "Yes, that sounds nice."

He pushed his mount forward, and Willow followed as they made their way down a small decline on the hill where even from where she sat, she could hear the tinkling sound of running water.

The stream was shallow, with round, pebbled rocks, some submerged, but most sitting just above the water's depth. Willow slid off her mount, throwing the reins over her horse's ears and tying them under its neck to stop the horse from stepping on it. She stood back, watching as both horses leaned down and nibbled on the grass before taking a drink.

The stream was narrow, with a large willow tree across the bank. Willow stepped into the water, ignoring the fact that her boots would be ruined after her little excursion.

The moment her foot stepped onto one of the smooth rocks, she knew she'd made a mistake. Her foot slipped out from beneath her, and she toppled, slipping forward. The ground rose quickly before her face, and she threw her hands out in front, wanting to protect herself as much as possible.

One would've hoped the godlike gentleman behind her would've reached out and plucked her from her impending doom. He did not. Instead, she landed with a splash, her gown instantly filled with chilling, cold water. She gasped, kneeling, checking her hands that stung like the devil.

"Willow," he shouted from behind.

Had it not occurred, Willow would never have believed it, but one moment she was kneeling in water, soaked through and decidedly embarrassed, and then next she was scooped up into the most muscular, warm arms she'd ever beheld. Her body sat nestled against his firm chest. Instantly her body sought his warmth, and she snuggled against him, taking the opportunity to revel in his hold while she could. It was unlikely that she would be in his arms again unless she started to feign falls all over the estate whenever he was about.

"Thank you," she said, surprised to hear her voice tremble a little. A shiver stole down her spine as he helped her to stand, rubbing her back vigorously to try to warm her.

"We should return to the house before you catch your death."

She nodded. He had the sweetest lips, or most sinful, she could not decide. What she did know was that he made her ache and shiver and long for things she knew nothing about. Something that she'd seen on occasion flicker within her friend's marriages. Willow had hoped for the same with her future husband, but alas, it would not be Lord Ryley. One had to protect oneself sometimes, and something about his lordship told Willow that to fall for the man before her would only end in heartbreak.

How many women had fallen at his knees, begging for another glance? How many had lain in his bed?

Too many to count.

His hands slowed on her back and she looked up to see his attention fully absorbed on her lips. Heat pooled in her core and her breath caught. Was he going to kiss her? "You have a mistress, my lord."

He stumbled back a step, his brow raised. "I beg your pardon."

She stepped back against him, clasping the lapels of his riding jacket. "Do you care for her? Enough that it will stop me from doing something that I've wanted to do for some time now."

He chuckled, but the slight tremor of nervousness could not be concealed. He was unsure. The thought was heady indeed. "No, but that does not mean I give you leave to do whatever it is that's circulating in that pretty head of yours."

His calling her pretty made her want to preen. She thought he was pretty too. Dangerous, but pretty. Willow took a determined breath, closed the space between them, and kissed him.

The word soft reverberated in her mind. Perfect, silky lips met hers, and her stomach roiled with longing. Never before had she ever kissed a man, and not just any man, but the Spanish Scoundrel. Unsure of what to do next, she pulled back, leaning on her tiptoes to kiss him again.

Still, he didn't move, simply stood there like a frozen statue one found in a museum. Willow chanced a look at him. His eyes burned with need, and she trembled. Would he kiss her back if she tried again? Something told her he would, but her nerve left her, and she stepped back.

"Oh no, you don't," he said, wrenching her against him, taking her mouth in a devastating kiss. A kiss that left her reeling and grappling for purpose. She gasped as his tongue slid against hers. "Oh," she murmured, having never felt anything so decadent in her life. His mouth worked hers, kissing her deep and pulling her tongue into a dance of desire.

He was as scandalous as he was rumored to be. He hauled her closer, his manhood pushing against her midriff, undulating and leaving heat to pool at her core. Fire blossomed over her skin, hot and prickly, and yet she could not stop. Could not get enough of him as he kissed her back, devoured her mouth as if she were the only thing keeping him alive.

His hands skimmed her back, lower still to cup her bottom, pulling her into his person.

Willow moaned as he dipped a bit, placing his manhood at the apex of her gown, pushing against a spot that no one other than herself had touched before. For all the times she had explored her own body, never had she been able to make herself feel the need that coursed through her now, making her mad with a longing that demanded satisfaction.

"Sweet. So damn sweet," he murmured against her lips, kissing her cheek, her neck and beyond. Trailing his tongue against the ridge of her breast. With nimble fingers, he flicked open her spencer, exposing her further to his touch.

Willow leaned her head back, more than willing to have him ravish her. If ravishment felt as good as she did right at this moment, she should've married a long time ago.

She ran her fingers through his hair, relishing the feel of his thick, black locks. Without thought, she undulated against him, spiking pleasure to her core. She moaned, the sound foreign and breathy. Suggestive.

His hand cupped her breast, squeezing it before he pulled her gown and bodice down, exposing her nipple. He ran his tongue over his lip, and she shivered, wanting his tongue on her. Her breathing ragged, she watched as he dipped his head, first kissing her breast before taking her nipple into his mouth.

"Oh, Lord Ryley," she gasped, holding him against her. Madness overcoming her. She should stop him. They should stop this right now, and yet she could not. Could only clutch at him and hope he'd never stop.

"Abe, call me Abe," he said, the breath of his words warm on her exposed skin.

"Abe," she breathed, giving herself over to him. Completely.

CHAPTER 7

*T*his was wrong. He was playing with fire, and he had no business doing what he was right at this moment with the delicious Miss Perry. Her nipple puckered in his mouth, and he gave it a teasing bite. She clutched at him, his to do what he wanted.

Here's your chance. Take her. Ruin her in this way and be done with it all. His name on her lips stopped him from picking her up, laying her on the bed of grass beside the small stream. That and the fact that the thumping of horse's hooves pounded against his conscience and the nearby turf.

He wrenched back, yanking up her gown and covering her breast. Her eyes wide and startled watched him, like a little bird that was certain it was about to be a cat's dinner. And Abe would've eaten her. Every last ounce of her skin he would've tasted, licked, savored.

She glanced toward the sound of Ava's return, more certain now, and quickly amended her hair, checking her riding attire. It was soaked through, dripping water at the hem, and yet, Abe was thankful for it. The disheveled appearance would give her cover for what had really tousled her person.

Him.

Ava came over the ridge, slowing her horse as she trotted toward them. "Here you are. I thought that you may have returned to the house." She was puffing from her ride, a light blush over her cheeks that matched the one of Miss Perry's. Abe reached out, offering his hand to the woman who left him entirely out of step.

"I fell over in the stream," Willow said to her friend, shrugging a little.

Ava chuckled, smiling at them, and thankfully not sensing anything untoward had occurred. "I'll have a bath readied for you on our return."

Abe inwardly groaned at the visual of Miss Perry naked in a bath, water cascading over her sweet breasts and cunny. "Let me help you mount, Miss Perry." She threw him a startled glance at his impatient request that was born out of frustration more than anything else.

She stepped out of the stream, and he cringed. He'd not even moved them from the water before he took advantage of her. Or had she taken advantage of him? She'd indeed kissed him first, had taken the opportunity while they were alone.

Not that he was complaining. He would kiss most women who offered themselves to him. He wasn't called the Spanish Scoundrel for nothing. He walked her to her horse, holding out his hand to hoist her atop the saddle.

She clutched the saddle and his shoulder and climbed on. The action gave him the most delightful glimpse of her derriere, and he took a calming breath, closing his eyes a moment to gather his spinning wits. The world wasn't the same, not after a kiss like that. His steps, more like strides toward his horse, didn't ease the need, the conflicting emotions that she wrought inside of him.

He hated her and her family.

Didn't he?

He was going to bring her down. Ruin her financially and now after that kiss, perhaps bodily as well.

Wasn't he?

Damn it. Abe hoisted himself upon his horse, waiting for the duchess and Miss Perry to precede him. They moved on, and he followed, not wanting to be part of their conversation. He was content to stay back, listen, and learn, plot his next step.

What that would be was anyone's guess. What he did know, however, was that one kiss would not divert him. After years of living without his mother, of having servants, stewards, and school headmasters raising him to be Marquess Ryley, he would not allow one kiss to throw him off. Make him question his morals.

He would need to start thinking with his mind more. Not his cock. Which right at this moment, was being led by a woman who had no business doing so.

~

*W*illow sat in the upstairs drawing room, waiting for Lord Ryley. He had summoned her here this afternoon to go over possible financial investments that she could invest in to grow her inheritance.

The idea of seeing him again left her all fidgety and not herself. There was something about him that made her want things no woman of good birth should. Not that she could attest to being born high on the social ladder, but she had been brought up with manners and just as groomed as a duke's daughter.

After their kiss yesterday, her mind had been reliving, relishing the memory of his touch. How he'd forcefully pulled down her bodice so his warm, wet lips could suckle her breast.

Heat pooled at her core, and she crossed her legs, wanting to soothe the ache he filled there. With a disgruntled huff, she stood, striding to the window. Whatever would she do? He was not a man looking for a wife. She should be pursuing Lord Herbert, who had arrived for dinner last evening and was now a neighbor to the duke and duchess here in Hampton. He seemed quite fond of her, very accommodating and handsome.

Not as handsome as Lord Ryley, but very few were.

Lord Ryley was dark, sinful, and with a face made for debauchery. She closed her eyes, her skin prickling in awareness.

The door opened, and she jumped, turning to see who had entered. Anticipation ran through her blood, and she crossed her arms, swallowing her nervousness.

Lord Ryley came into the room and, spying her, shut the door and bowed. "Miss Perry. Shall we?" He gestured toward the desk that sat at the end of the room.

"Of course," she said, joining him. The desk had numerous books and papers, most comprising horse sketches and books on horse breeding and training manuals. This desk was most definitely Ava's little domain, or at least she had taken claim of the space.

His lordship sat and folded his hands before him, his gaze somewhere over her shoulder.

Willow frowned. Was he not going to look her directly

in the eye? She watched him, her temper rising a little at his indifference to her. She would see about that!

He opened a folder that sat before him, lifting out a piece of parchment and placing it before her. "Here are some of the options I thought may be open to your deliberation. Some are based on mining here in England and Cornwall, coal mines to be precise. The second option is investing in cargo ships that travel to and from the West Indies or Jamaica. They deal in oil, salted skins, fur, sugar, that sort of cargo. You could of course invest in both if it pleased you."

Willow read over the neat script, the details of the mines, and the ships that would sail from London to Jamaica and beyond. She glanced at him, narrowing her eyes when again he watched something over her shoulder. Willow moved to the side, dipping her head to catch his gaze.

He relented, and triumph drummed through her when at last, she made him look at her, except her award was short-lived. His gaze was heavy, dangerous, and consumed her, making her mind blank regarding everything they were discussing.

How could he strip her bare, with only a look? Make her skin hot and clammy. Her female brain lose all concentration. "What do you suggest I choose?" she asked, not caring which one she invested in so long as he kept looking at her as he now was.

"The coal mine in Cornwall would be a good investment. I have money going into it as well."

She glanced back down at the report, her mind scrambling to make sense of what was happening between them. Willow bit her lip. Was this how rakes looked at women they wanted to bed? Was how Lord Ryley was looking at her how he looked at his lovers?

"You never answered my question yesterday," she blurted. The moment the words left her lips, she wanted to rip them back. But also, another part of her wanted to know the answer to her question. Before, he'd deliciously distracted her with his mouth.

He leaned back in his chair. Even from where she sat, she could see he debated telling her the truth. His gaze slid over her, and her skin prickled in awareness. Her breasts felt heavy and large, as if they were longing for his touch, his mouth once again.

Willow took a calming breath, clutching her hands in her lap to stop them from fiddling with anything.

"I have a mistress who lives with me. Are you glad to hear the truth?"

Willow wasn't glad at all to hear such things. He lived with his lover? Her mind screamed to get away from the man before her. While her body longed for his touch, to make him want her as much as she wanted him.

His jaw clenched before he swore, standing and coming around the desk. He wrenched her out of her chair and kissed her. Hard. Willow fought to keep her footing, to keep upright at the onslaught of his mouth.

She fell into the kiss, having missed his touch the moment he stepped away from her the day before. This is what she wanted. She wanted to live, to love and learn the ways of the woman, and she wanted to do all of that in this man's arms. If she were going to marry, what better way to learn the art of being a wife than in the arms of a rake?

At least by being tutored by such a proficient lover her

husband would never stray. Would love and cherish her and no one else for the rest of their days.

His tongue fought with hers, and she threw herself into the embrace. The kiss was madness, a melding of mouths that was untutored and hard. The thought that he kissed his mistress like this doused her desire, and she pushed him away, moving out of his reach.

"You have a mistress and you're kissing me. What they say about you really is true, isn't it?"

He threw her a wolfish grin. Heat pooled between her legs, and she cursed him his good, undeniable looks. "Of course. I'll never be tamed, my dear. Not by anyone."

Willow reached around him, scooping up the papers and holding them against her chest. "I will look over these suggestions and get back to you."

He bowed, stepping aside to let her pass. "Of course. Let me know when you're ready to invest."

His deep, wicked chuckle followed her out the door.

~

*T*he following evening Ava had decided on an impromptu night of dancing. They were all gathered in the sizable ballroom, musicians having traveled up from London to play for them all. The duke had invited some friends from London. With their new estate so close to town, it was an easy distance to travel.

Willow stood to the side of the room, no sign of Lord Ryley, which suited her just fine. He was maddening if ever there were a man who was so. She spotted Ava talking to the tall and handsome Lord Herbert, her friend casting her amused glances every so often.

What was she up to? Lord Herbert glanced at her, and

73

Willow studied him a moment. He was tall, blond, and the opposite of how Lord Ryley appeared. If Lord Ryley was dark and sinful, this gentleman looked light and pure. He had an air of innocence, much more suited to the future she'd planned to have.

Would he be different from all the other gentlemen who kept mistresses on the side? That was yet to be determined. Willow inwardly cringed when Ava started toward her, Lord Herbert at her side.

"Willow, let me formally introduce you to Lord Herbert. Lord Herbert, this is my friend, Miss Willow Perry."

She dipped into a curtsy, and he bowed. "Miss Perry, lovely to make your acquaintance once again."

His voice was smooth, pleasant, safe. "It's good of you to come. I hear that you're neighbors to the duke and duchess here in Hampton."

"I am." He grinned, and Willow had to admit that he was charming, at least at the moment. Ava excused herself and he turned to her. "I understand you went to school with the duchess."

"I did." She smiled at the reminder of their school years, the antics and sneaking out that they tried whenever the possibility presented itself. Of how they all dreamed of their futures and what they entailed. To be where she was now, an heiress was not what she ever thought would happen. "She is one of the best people I know."

Lord Herbert glanced in the direction Ava had gone. "I agree. The duke and duchess are honorable."

"Have you known them long?" she asked.

"Since Cambridge with the duke. I've not known you for long, however, but I'd like to change that."

She glanced at him, surprised at his boldness. "You

do?" She narrowed her eyes on him, debating if he were worth the effort. He raised his brow, his blue eyes dancing with amusement.

"I do if you're willing, of course." He glanced at the dancing couples. "Will you dance with me, Miss Perry?"

Without thought, she placed her hand on his arm, nodding. "Thank you, yes." He pulled her onto the floor, and she laughed as he twirled her into his arms. Perhaps this man was worth a little trouble. She was looking for love, for someone who would be faithful to her. Maybe Lord Herbert was that man. Lord Ryley certainly was not. That fiend hadn't even bothered to turn up yet.

CHAPTER 8

*A*be had ridden hard from London with the need to return to the duke and duchess's new estate, especially after he'd received a summons not to miss their dance they'd decided to host. He'd needed to return to town and check on the Hell's Gate. Tonight they were hosting a gambling event that had card players not only from England but abroad. He'd put up a large winning to those who registered, and the interest had been extensive.

That his oldest friend and his wife had decided to host a dance on the same night was bothersome but would not impact him too much. He had a team of people who were more than capable of handling the night. He could spend the evening with his friends.

He jumped off his horse at the front of the house, handing his mount to a waiting stable boy. He shucked out of his greatcoat, hat, and gloves, handing them over to the footman in the foyer, not bothering to go upstairs to change. All day, a nagging feeling of impending doom had crawled over his skin. Something was amiss.

What was amiss was evident the moment he stepped

into the ballroom. His lip curled. He should have expected to see what he now saw. Lord Perfect—or known within their society as Lord Herbert. A friend of the duke since before Abe started at Eton.

Lord Herbert was always eager to please during his school years. Willing to tell on anyone should he think they were doing wrong or he could get ahead by such information. As a grown man, he wasn't much different. Always sickly sweet to the opposite sex, keen to tell them what they wanted to hear and rumor had it, he was after a wife.

Miss Perry fitted his lordship's requirements perfectly. She was looking for a husband, was rich enough to satisfy the family, and for them to overlook her common heritage.

If she were to marry Lord Perfect, his revenge on the Vances would impact the Herberts also. A satisfying idea since it was Lady Herbert, Lord Perfect's mother, who had helped Viscountess Vance ruin his mama.

His conscience pricked at the thought of hurting Willow. Depending on how much he could persuade her to invest would depend on how much she fell from grace. A large sum could mean the loss of her Hanover Square home. Minimal staff and possibly having to find employment as a companion or lady's maid.

He stepped into the room, heading toward the Duchess of Whitstone and his friend Viscount Duncannon. He threw appreciative glances toward the women who looked his way, winking at Lady Sussex, who blushed and giggled like a young girl in her presenting year.

Thankfully he had a mistress, and his days of having to seduce married or widowed women were behind him unless they were unwilling to take no for an answer.

He never liked to leave anyone unsatisfied.

Abe glanced over to where he'd seen Miss Perry last

and caught sight of her stepping onto the dancefloor with Lord Perfect. He procured a glass of wine from a passing footman and continued, dodging the guests as he went.

"Duchess. Duncannon," he said, coming up to them and taking a fortifying sip of his drink. "What is Lord Perfect doing here? I would not think a sojourn into the country was his pleasure when there was more to be had flattering the ladies in London."

Duncannon chuckled, throwing him an amused look. The duchess whacked his chest with her fan. "Behave, Ryley. You know as well as I there is nothing wrong with Lord Herbert." She smiled at the gentleman as he pulled Miss Perry into a waltz.

Willow's laughter carried over to him, and he watched them. Her ease within the man's arms made his skin crawl.

"That is your opinion, and you are welcome to it, Your Grace." As for his opinion, he wanted to pummel the man into a pulp. His gaze narrowed in on Lord Perfect's hand. A hand that was far too low on Miss Perry's back.

"Miss Perry looks beautiful this evening. Her newfound independence suits her." Duncannon smiled at Ava and met Abe's eyes over the duchess's head, laughter lurking in his blue orbs. Abe did not appreciate the mocking.

"She does, doesn't she? I'm so glad her aunt thought of her and her security after her death. And did you hear, Duncannon that the wonderful Lord Ryley is going to help her with some investments? Are you not, my lord?"

Abe nodded, guilt creeping up his spine at the duchess's faith in him. "I have supplied her with suggestions. The choice as to what she invests in is up to her." Not that he'd given her high odds in earning back her investment. In fact, all the options he'd told her to consider were likely to fail and take down any investors who were foolish enough to put money into them.

He drank down the last of his wine. Revenge was never pretty, and his mother deserved the respect that was denied her. He would take down the family that ruined her name in London and push aside the fact that Miss Perry had not been part of that plot. Not physically, but she was a blood relative, and the only one left. He would make them all pay.

That his mother had fled England, leaving him behind to face their taunts at school, Lord Perfect was kind to the boys he deemed his equal, but not Ryley. He had English and Spanish blood in his veins and was a lesser person in his lordship's eyes. The child had learned well from his sires, but Ryley was no longer the boy who had to fend off such insults. No longer in need of anyone's approval. He was wealthy beyond his means, women flocked to him, and men wanted to be in his inner circle.

The Lord Perfects of the world could go hang and their trouble-making parents along with them.

The duchess moved away, and Duncannon studied him a moment. "I've seen that look before. You have the visage of a man about to commit murder."

Abe took a calming breath, knowing the fact that Miss Perry danced with a man he loathed was not Duncannon's fault. His friend didn't deserve a sharp retort. "I don't understand why Lord Perfect would be invited in all honesty. We've never been friends, and the duke knows that. Perhaps he ought not to have invited me."

"No," Duncannon said, frowning. "Whitstone is loyal to you. I believe they invited him because he is their neighbor here in Hampton. Although, between you and me, I do believe they're trying to source a husband for Miss Perry."

"And they think Lord Perfect would do admirably. He's a popinjay and an ass. Two characteristics I wouldn't think are sought after in a gentleman."

Duncannon chuckled. "It is good then that you're not seeking a husband."

Abe refused to comment on such a statement. The situation was not at all amusing.

"Come now, Ryley. Even you must admit that he would suit Miss Perry. He's wealthy himself, so we know he is not hunting her fortune. He's merely ready to settle."

The word settle rankled. Abe watched as Miss Perry floated about the floor, seemingly enjoying her waltz with a man who made Abe seethe. The thought of Miss Perry settling with anyone didn't sit well either. Why, however, he could not say or certainly would not venture to understand. He was simply addled of mind after their two kisses. The memory of which made him burn and seethe in equal measure.

He called over a footman, taking two glasses of brandy. "Let him marry her. Maybe if the bastard is leg shackled, he'll fuck off out of London, and I'll never have to see him again." Abe clapped Duncannon on the back, ignoring his friend's shock at his words. "Now, let's get drunk."

~

*W*illow snuck outside onto the terrace and away from the impromptu ball a little while after supper. The air was fresh, just the slightest chill that made her skin prickle. She took a deep breath, basking in the tranquil space and the fresh country air that smelled of grass and flowers.

Taking in the terrace, and spying no one outside, she strolled its length, looking out over the grounds, which were lit with burning oil lanterns.

Footsteps sounded behind her, and she turned. A small jab of disappointment marking her when she spied Lord Herbert seeking her out.

"Miss Perry, are you well? I saw you leave, and I was concerned."

She shook her head. He really was a caring gentleman like Ava had said he was. "Oh no, I'm perfectly well, thank you. I just needed some fresh air. Even though the ball is not large by London standards, the room has grown quite stuffy."

"I agree," he said, leaning against the terrace railing. "I have been away from England for some months, having only returned recently. May I say now that we're alone that I was saddened to hear of your aunt's passing. She was a close friend of my mother. I believe they had their coming out the same year."

"Really," Willow said, having not known that. She studied him anew. If her aunt had been friends with his family, he could not be a rogue or scoundrel looking to ruin her or marry her for her money. Perhaps his interest in her was honorable, and he was looking for a wife. "I did not know that, my lord."

"Yes." He smiled, and she had to admit he was very handsome. A lovely, wide smile and eyes that appeared kind and attentive. And yet even with all of these positives, there was nothing. Nothing fluttered in her stomach, nothing yearned or longed within her whenever he looked at her. She may as well have been looking at a brick wall for all the emotions he stirred inside. "Viscountess Vance and her friendship throughout the years have been a comfort to my mother."

Willow smiled, knowing that her aunt, for all her sometimes opinionated ideals was kind at heart and always meant well. "She is missed to be sure. I'm glad you told me they were friends, perhaps we can be too."

He reached out, picking up her hand and bringing it to his lips. She prayed his kiss atop her glove would stir something, anything within her, but it did not. Willow inwardly sighed.

"Here is to our new friendship and possibly more." He grinned, and Willow smiled, her amusement slipping when she spied another lord coming onto the terrace. Or perhaps, stumbling onto the terrace would be a better term.

She stepped back, and Lord Herbert turned, facing Lord Ryley. The Spanish Scoundrel took in them both, the disgust at finding them together written clearly on his face.

He was drunk, a little less pristine to how he usually dressed, and she swallowed, hating that the mere sight of him made her blood pump fast in her veins. Made her skin prickle in awareness. Would he tell Lord Herbert of their kisses? The memory of which made her stomach twist into delicious knots. She licked her lips, scandalous as it may be, wanting to know what he tasted like when in his cups.

"Lord Ryley. Always a pleasure." Lord Herbert's tone seethed with sarcasm and distaste, and Willow took in both gentlemen. They glared at each other, reminding her of two dogs snarling and growling before a fight. Beneath all their finery, there was a core of hatred that was as palatable as the dress she wore this evening.

They hated each other, and it was an old hatred, not because of her, she would guess.

A little part of her was thankful for that. Another part couldn't help but wish that there were two lords as handsome as these two were who were fighting to win her hand. Her love.

Lord Ryley would scoff at the notion. He was decidedly not looking for love. Lust and sex drove that gentleman, and she would no longer be part of that. Two kisses were quite enough. It was time for her to find a man who would love her, who she could grow to love, and have a happy life. A man like Lord Herbert, for instance.

She pushed away the disappointment that Lord Ryley would never be the man for her. The Spanish Scoundrel was not marriageable material.

"Lord Perfect, I see you weaseled your way into receiving an invitation. How delightful to see you again."

Willow glanced at Lord Ryley, his tone just as sarcastic and lacking emotion as Lord Herbert's. And who was Lord Perfect? She cleared her throat, bringing Lord Ryley's attention to her. There was something about the way Lord Ryley was looking at Lord Herbert that gave her pause. If she were a betting man, she would say that he wanted to throttle his lordship. Whatever had happened between them to cause such hatred?

"I could say the same for you. Why are you not in your gambling den with the rest of the uncouth?" Lord Herbert stepped back, coming to stand at her side, watching Lord Ryley.

Lord Ryley took them in, his gaze landing on Willow and not shifting. She shivered under his inspection, the emotions that she hadn't felt earlier with Lord Herbert pumping through her like blood. Her body trembled and clenched, her stomach twisting pleasantly.

None of it would do. Lord Ryley would dally with her and leave her to rot after he'd taken his fill. She could not allow herself to fall under his wicked spell no matter how tempting the thought of it was. No matter how attractive the memory of his mouth moving over hers, his tongue sliding and invading her mouth was.

"Jealous you've never been there." Lord Ryley chuckled, the sound menacing. "I wouldn't think a gambling hell was a place Lord Perfect hankered to call upon."

"I've asked you repeatedly not to call me that," Lord Herbert said just before Willow was about to ask who Lord Ryley meant.

"Gentlemen, please. I think name-calling is a little juvenile, don't you agree?"

"I never insulted the Spanish Scoundrel."

Lord Ryley raised his brow. "Have you not? I recall it differently."

They stared at each other, and Willow looked between them. Two bulls facing off from each other before they charged. "Shall we return indoors?"

Lord Ryley relented first, surprising Willow. He moved aside, gesturing for them to pass. Willow started toward the house, Lord Herbert by her side.

"Miss Perry, may I have a word before you return indoors?" Lord Ryley asked. His lordship glowered at Lord Herbert. "In private."

"It isn't proper for Miss Perry to be out here with you," Lord Herbert threw down, glaring at Lord Ryley.

Willow patted his lordship on the arm, gaining his attention. "I was safe with you, my lord. I shall be just as safe with Lord Ryley. I will return indoors directly."

He didn't move for a moment, and Willow wondered if he'd protest, but then on a sigh, he nodded and stepped back through the terrace doors, leaving her decidedly alone with Lord Ryley.

"What is it you wished to speak to me about?" she asked.

He leaned on the terrace railing, studying her with a quietness that left her discombobulated. How was it that a simple look was enough to make her nerves sizzle? How was it that a man she hardly knew could affect her so? It was disturbing and delicious all at the same time.

"Nothing at all. I merely wanted to separate you from Lord Perfect. I always get what I want, Miss Perry. Even at the expense of others at times."

She huffed out a disgruntled breath, fisting her hands at her sides. "You're impossible." She started over to him, stopping a mere breath from his face. "I'm not your toy, and you playing with me before others is not acceptable. I was enjoying my time with Lord Herbert and you put a stop to that simply because you dislike the gentleman?"

He nodded once. "I did. I don't merely dislike him. I loathe him and his kind. Just like his mother, he's a nasty, conniving, gossiping prick."

Willow gasped, having never heard a man speak about another in such a crude way before. The hatred was old, and if she understood anything about Lord Ryley, which wasn't a lot, it was that a wound festered and rotted his core.

"Whatever you feel for Lord Herbert I can see it eats at you. Simply by the way you speak. You need to move on from whatever it was that he offended you with, or one day you'll look up, and no one will be around you who cares."

His lip curled in a snarl, and she took a step back. "Ah,

but that's just it, my sweet Miss Perry. I do not care if no one is around to console me and my festering wound. If they walk from my life, they were never friends to begin with. And a word of advice, my dear. Do not talk to me as if you know anything about why I hate Lord Herbert. The wound is deep, but I shall have my revenge, you should heed my warning and take care."

She shook her head, his words not making any sense. "What do you mean by that? Why should I take care?"

"If you associate yourself with his lordship, you may be tainted by association. A friend of his is an enemy of mine."

"So, we're enemies now?" She took another step closer. It was wrong of her, but his scent of sandalwood and something uniquely Lord Ryley pulled her in. The memory of his mouth on hers, commanding a response that drew her in and made her yearn for more. "We were not so the other day," she said, hoping he'd remember their kiss, even in his drunken state.

His gaze dipped to her lips and a shiver wracked her spine. "No, we were not."

～

*H*er mouth, the memory of her kiss, almost undid Abe. He held on to the balustrade, fighting the urge to wrench her up against him and take her perfect, sweet mouth with his. He'd been uncommonly rude, arrogant, and cutting to her this evening, but seeing her with Lord Perfect had snapped some invisible thread that was holding his two halves together.

He shouldn't care what the chit did. She could go on and marry whomever she wanted, someone safe and spineless like Lord Perfect. All tormentors were of such caliber. Even so, the thought of Miss Perry marrying such a man left a sour taste in his mouth. The idea of her in another man's bed made his blood boil.

Damn the wench and her wiles. Her ability to get under his skin must be a trait she'd earned being related to Viscountess Vance. That woman could always raise his hackles whenever he saw her.

"If you can give me a reason as to why I should keep away from Lord Herbert. A sensible reason, not some boyhood hatred you've refused to let go, I may do as you heed."

Abe listened halfheartedly to what Miss Perry said, his attention in his whiskey-fogged mind had diverted to her gown. The deep-pink satin suited her golden locks. The bodice hugged her ample bosom, and her slim waist was accentuated by the drop of the empire-style gown. The little cuff sleeves on her shoulder outlined her slender frame, the skin between where her gloves ended and her gown began begging for a kiss. His mouth.

"My lord? Did you hear anything that I just said?" she asked, catching his gaze.

With every morsel of control, he pushed off from the terrace railing, righting his cravat. "If he pleases you, by all means, marry him. It means nothing to me." He slipped past her, but she clasped his arm, halting him.

He stared down at her delicate hand, not quite believing she'd manhandled him into stopping.

"You're a terrible liar, Lord Ryley. And you know I know it."

He huffed out a laugh, harsh and condescending, hating the fact that a little part of him, a piece he didn't want to acknowledge, knew she was right. He didn't like the idea of her power over his person. Not a bloody bit.

"You don't know anything about me, other than the fact that I've taken advantage of you twice by kissing you. Do not read into my actions any more than what they are. I'm not for you, Miss Perry." He wasn't for anyone. What he needed was to return to London so the woman before him would stop bothering him so much. Saying things about him that he had to deny while knowing deep down what she said was the truth.

For all his ideals of bringing this woman down, of ruining her, there was something about her that thwarted his plan. Her ease with others, the fact that she had not had everything handed to her like so many of his ilk pulled at his honorable cord.

He reminded himself he'd been raised without parents solely due to Miss Perry's aunt and Lord Perfect's mother. Servants and a tutor were the only security he'd had for years. His unhappy childhood could be laid at Miss Perry's feet and her family.

She watched him, her eyes bright with pity and regret. He'd have none of that. No one looked down at him, not for anything. He glanced at her hand before she became aware of her hold on him. She released him, but not before he read the awareness that ran through her. It vibrated through him as well. An unusual reaction that he'd never had with another woman before. He'd felt the rush of emotion for an impending shag, the desire as his mistress brought him to release, but never had he merely been within the same room as a woman and had his prick stand to attention.

Like it did now beside Miss Perry.

He leaned toward her, almost nose to nose. "I may not

be suitable for a husband, but I'm more than happy to accommodate you in other ways. More pleasurable ways if you're so inclined."

Her mouth opened and need seized him. Damn her for being sweet enough to pluck. The memory of waking up in his large London home at the tender age of six years to see his mother's trunks being loaded onto a carriage floated through his mind. He'd begged her to stay, had clutched at her dress, and wailed at the idea of not seeing her again. It would be another twelve years before he did see her again, and that was in Spain where she lived.

She was happy there, had made a life for herself. One consolation he supposed.

Abe stepped back, starting for the door. He would not give in to her charms. She was a Vance. His enemy. She was allowing Lord Perfect to court her. Another enemy. There was no way in hell he'd let himself fall under her charm. No matter how beautiful, how loyal she seemed to be to her friends.

She was not for him.

"Have a pleasant evening, Miss Perry. I wish you well in landing your Lord Perfect." Abe stormed toward the door, ignoring her shocked gasp behind him. He wasn't called the Spanish Scoundrel for nothing.

CHAPTER 9

*T*he next afternoon Willow sat and took tea with Lord Perfect. She frowned at her lapse in concentration and amended her thoughts to that of Lord Herbert. Lord Ryley and his inappropriate opinions on his lordship were wiggling their way into her mind and muddling her thoughts.

The gentleman wasn't too perfect. He was kind and knowledgeable, and from what he stated about his estates, was not after a wealthy wife. He seemed well-positioned to look after his affairs.

She took a sip of her sweet tea, watching him over the brim of the cup. He was discussing his estate here in Hampton, the extent and how many tenant farms he had. It was a sizable asset, or at least Willow thought it was. All she could hope was that his marked attention on her was heartfelt, and he wasn't playing her a fool.

Lord Ryley had not told her exactly why he disliked the man so much, but that Whitstone was his friend surely meant he wasn't so very bad. For all Willow knew, Lord

Herbert may have cut Lord Ryley out of a possible mistress or won a game of high-stakes cards, fleecing him of funds.

"Do you have any plans for this afternoon, Miss Perry? I do believe the weather will be fine from what I could deem earlier for a ride."

Willow glanced out the window and caught sight of Lord Ryley talking to Whitstone out on the terrace outside. Nerves pooled in her stomach, and she tore her gaze back to Lord Herbert, not needing the distraction that his lordship wrought on her every time she saw him. Vexing man.

"I wanted to walk the grounds and catch up on some reading before the entertainments tonight. I do believe the duchess has some games planned for us."

Laughter caught their attention, and Lord Herbert glanced toward the terrace, his eyes narrowing on the duke. He turned back to her, watching her closely.

"Have you known Lord Ryley for long, Miss Perry?"

She shook her head. "Not at all. He is only a recent acquaintance."

"Hmmm," his lordship murmured. "I thought after his intrusion upon us last evening that perhaps I was stepping into a situation that I should not be part of."

Heat rushed onto her cheeks, and she sipped her tea to bide her time before answering. She had kissed Lord Ryley with abandon. Wantonly she'd allowed him favors that she should not have. The memory of his mouth on her breast ought to scandalize her. Make her feel uncouth and wanton, but it did not. If anything, her body simmered with awakening. A curiosity to learn what else he could make her feel. Which, unfortunately, was so very different from what Lord Herbert made her feel.

"Of course not. We simply have mutual friends, and he

was concerned for my reputation being outside with a gentleman. That was all."

"If only it were the case," Lord Herbert said, placing down his cup of tea and leaning back in his chair, folding his legs. "May I speak frank, Miss Perry?"

Willow glanced about them, ensuring they were quite out of hearing of others before nodding. "Of course. Please."

He threw her a small smile before he said, "I want you to know that I'm at that stage in my life that I'm ready to settle down. Marry and start a family. You have probably heard this rumor about London or this house party, but I wanted to let you know that it is true."

Willow swallowed a sip of tea, having not expected him to be so forward, even so, it was refreshing that a gentleman was telling her the truth of his situation and not merely eluding to it like so many of them did. "I wish you good luck in finding your future wife, my lord."

He chuckled. "I want you to know that no matter what anyone may say," he said, glancing at Lord Ryley. "I am honorable and would never play anyone a fool. I would never lead any woman to believe I felt more for them than I did."

"That is an honorable trait to have, my lord. Thank you for telling me so."

"I tell you this because I do not wish for your good opinion of me to be sullied by Lord Ryley. I know it is wrong of me to name him so publicly to you, but his hatred of me is of long duration and somewhat jaded. He knows not what he speaks."

Willow narrowed her eyes at his lordship, before glancing at Lord Ryley. He looked up from talking to Whitstone, and their gazes clashed. Her skin prickled, and her heart thumped loud in her chest at his lordship's seductive, dark gaze. She wrenched her attention back to Lord Herbert, ignoring the all-consuming man in her peripheral vision.

"Lord Ryley has not spoken ill of you," she lied, not wanting to further the rift that seemed to be between the gentlemen.

"That is sweet of you to say, but I know he dislikes me, and over the years, his actions within society have made me possibly dislike him just as much. We are not friends, nor will we ever be, but I hope that does not impact our friendship. I would like to get better acquainted if you're willing."

Was she willing? Before her sat a man who encumbered all that she was looking for in a husband. He was kind, well-respected by those closest to her in all the world. He was wealthy and titled, and so could not be termed a fortune hunter. Handsome too, with his dark-blue eyes and blond locks that were short and well-trimmed.

He may not light a fire in her soul, but maybe that would come in time. If he kissed her, perhaps then that would spark a reaction within her, similar to what occurred with Lord Ryley. She would not know until she tried.

"I would like that very much, my lord."

He threw her a broad smile and she felt a little giddy at his interest in her. She would give Lord Herbert time and see. To throw him over for Lord Ryley simply because his lordship had kissed her first was no reason at all not to see if someone else may suit her better.

Lord Ryley was not the marrying type. He was the type who stormed through a courtship, spinning everyone and leaving those affected by him heartbroken in his wake. She didn't wish to be left heartbroken by him. Ruined and left without a backward glance when something else more interesting, more alluring came along.

He'd said himself he wasn't made to be a husband, and she wouldn't try and make him into something he did not want to be. He would only end up resenting her, and that would never be palatable to her. A future with Lord Ryley was unattainable, but a future with Lord Herbert was a possibility. She would be a simpleton indeed to push him away just because Lord Ryley's kisses were so delectably naughty.

"Maybe this afternoon on your walk, I may join you?" he asked sweetly.

Willow could feel the heat of Lord Ryley's gaze on her, but she refused to look at him. He was an error of judgment on her behalf, a slip of common sense that thankfully had righted itself before too much damage was made. Lord Herbert, on the other hand, was safe, sweet, and willing to see where their courtship could take them. A much better option for her. "I would like that, my lord. Shall we meet on the terrace outside the library after luncheon?"

"I look forward to it, Miss Perry."

$\sim$

Their afternoon stroll had been pleasant. They had talked about London, her plans going forward, her desire to travel abroad, where Willow was doubly pleased to hear that Lord Herbert too was looking to travel in the next year or so.

Willow found they both liked horses, lived not far from each other in London. As they strolled the grounds of the duke and duchess's new estate, looking at the plants and the small stream that ran through the property, she could not fathom as to why Lord Ryley disliked the gentleman so much. He certainly seemed harmless. That his mother had been best friends with her aunt had put her mind at ease over his character. Even though she could not recall seeing her aunt and his mother together much in society.

Could the friendship have cooled a little over time? Or was it that their lives had simply moved in different directions? "You said that your mother was close to my aunt, and yet I rarely saw them in town together. Please tell me if I'm overstepping my bounds, but do you know why that was the case?"

Lord Herbert frowned, and she marveled at how handsome he was. Not in the dark, brooding kind of way Lord Ryley was, but in an ethereal, godlike way instead. Where Lord Ryley was dark, Lord Herbert was light. It was probably why she had gravitated toward Lord Ryley in the first place. A dark god, full of shadows and trickery always fooled its prey into believing they were something they were not.

Lord Ryley would no longer outwit her.

"You are right. They were not as close as they once were. I suppose their lives took them in different directions and social spheres. My mother, as you know, married an earl, but because they debuted the same year, they were always friends and did try to see each other as much as events allowed."

They strolled along, and Willow stared down at the grassy, soft lawn beneath her slippers. The air smelled of fresh pine and flowers, a light, cooling breeze took the sting out of the day's heat. Ava's new estate was very picturesque, and as they came around the west side of the house, they caught sight of the stables and new racing track Ava would use to train her horses.

"Understandable of course. My aunt only married a viscount, and I suppose even that rank can cause a chasm to open up between friends." Willow caught sight of Ava atop a horse, the duke at her side, glancing up at her with adoration. She hoped that her friendship with Ava and Hallie would not cease because they were now both titled and far above her, Evie, and Molly in rank. They had been friends for so many years, and she didn't know what she would do if she lost them.

His lordship strolled beside her, his arms clasped behind his back. She studied him a moment. "My friendships with Ava, Hallie, Evie, and Molly are the most important friendships of my life. No matter whom I marry, I shall never allow rank or wealth or opinions to come between that bond." Willow raised her chin, needing his lordship to know that should he ask her and she decided to marry his lordship, become a countess, she would not allow anyone, or any of his circle to influence or stop her friendship with Evie and Molly. Should either of her friends marry even a clergyman or gentleman farmer, she would continue to invite and love them as much as she did now, and the *ton* could go hang if it did not like it.

"That is a noble ideal, Miss Perry, but society has a way sometimes of coming between even the strongest of friendships."

Willow smiled noncommittedly and started toward where the duke stood watching Ava ride. "Shall we join Whitstone before we return indoors? Perhaps he can tell us a little more about these games that the duchess has in store for us all. She's been very secretive and will not say a word about it," she said, wanting to end their little stroll together. That he'd said what he did about her friendships rattled her. For all his kindness, his gentlemanly behavior, his words left her cold. Would he expect her to leave her friendship with Evie and Molly behind because of their position? It wasn't to be borne, but then, maybe he was speaking in general terms, not of what his own opinion was on the matter.

As they came up to the duke, she smiled in welcome and was pleased that the gentlemen became engrossed in talk of horses and the breeding of them. Willow slipped away unnoticed, needing the sanctity of her room. Why did having to find a husband have to be so very confusing and vexing? She was starting to think this whole idea of marriage was an absurd notion that was too much work.

And not the least worth the effort.

CHAPTER 10

*A*be had given Miss Perry some space over the last few days, but with each passing moment, the marked attention of Lord Herbert had started to irk. Why, he couldn't fathom. He didn't want to marry the chit. He didn't want to marry anyone.

His mother's parting words before she fled to Spain were to be careful of who he gave his heart to. She could have only meant one thing by that. That she'd given her heart to his father, and in her time of need, when she had needed him to stand up with her against those who ridiculed and taunted her, he had not.

Up to this time in his life, Abe had not felt the smallest inclination to give his heart to anyone. To let another in to know all his dark, ugly secrets. Until Miss Perry, that was.

Abe started at the thought, running a hand through his hair. What the blazes was he talking about? He didn't feel anything beyond mild amusement with Miss Perry. For all her pretty looks and ample bank balance, she held no special place in his life.

Did she?

He swore, storming, more than strolling toward the stables. He stood corrected. She wasn't just amusement, she was the sole reason he was out in the country for a blasted week. He needed her to sign off on a specific investment that would hurt her financially.

Abe had decided that he'd not let her invest all her money. He wasn't that much of an ass, but he would have her spend enough that it would require adjustments to her household.

His friends, if they found out what he intended, would call him a bastard, and maybe he was. But the Vance family was cruel, unforgivingly bitter toward his mother, and he'd not let them get away with it. The old Viscountess Vance had been crafty with loyal accountants who had not seen fit to invest in anything, but Miss Perry was different. From his investigations into her, he'd found out she had hired her own solicitor, more modern and forward-thinking than her late aunt's.

Solicitors who were easily persuaded into foolhardy investments suggested by a peer of the realm.

Abe came to an abrupt halt at the sight of Miss Perry walking arm in arm in the gardens with Lord Herbert. The pompous lord smiled down at her and even Abe had to admit that he looked genuine with his interest.

He wouldn't let that bastard have her either. Lord Herbert always managed to get what he wanted, but not anymore. He would too have his day, and at the hands of Abe, he would ensure that.

For the life of him, he could not see what Miss Perry saw in the pretentious fool. Lord Perfect, who didn't step out of line or do anything that went against his mother's will. If Miss Perry wished to marry into that lofty family, she would have to impress the old battleax. Women from far wealthier families than hers and with loftier connections had failed.

He stopped, debating with himself whether he'd interrupt them or not. To anyone watching his actions, he'd look like a besotted fool who'd had his love interest swooped out from beneath his grasp.

There was a first for everything, but he'd be damned if he'd let Lord Perfect have Miss Perry. Not that he wanted her from himself. Blast it, no, he did not, but the fiend currently walking with her, glancing down at her as if the sun shone out of her preverbal ass would not do either.

"Something amiss, Ryley?" Duncannon said behind him, startling him from his inspection.

Duncannon was a good friend, loyal to a fault at times, but could read him like a book, and there was little point in disassembling. "I'm vexed, damn it, and Miss Perry is the reason behind my ire." He started toward the stables again, Duncannon hard on his heels.

"Willow? What has she done to you, old boy?"

Abe halted, Duncannon running into him, sending him tumbling forward. Willow? Duncannon called her by her given name. He turned slowly, unsure what the emotions that were rioting about inside him meant by knowing they were on such intimate terms. "You call her by her given name, and your wife approves?"

Duncannon stared at him, eyes narrowing as he understood his anger. "I call all of my wife's friends by their given names most of the time. Has the fact that Miss Perry has not given you leave to use her name annoyed you, my friend?" Duncannon's knowing chuckle followed him, spiking his temper.

"Your mockery makes me question our friendship and what the hell I'm doing here."

"Wait," Duncannon said, clasping his arm. "This is more than Miss Perry not giving you leave to use her name. You're jealous of Herbert."

"The hell I am," Abe sneered. "And anyway, what is he doing here? You know what I think of him."

Duncannon frowned, sighing. "Lord Herbert is only here because Whitstone does not like to cause trouble. You know we're loyal to you, have your back. There are many in attendance that we do not court close friendship with. Why this overreaction?" Duncannon held him fast, his grip tight on his arm. "You like Miss Perry. You like her more than you're even allowing yourself to admit."

"I absolutely do not," he stated, his voice curt and final. A lie upon his lips that tasted sour and wrong. He did like her. Liked her more than he'd let anyone know, even himself. Why, though, was the question? Was it because she was forbidden to him due to her family being his enemy? Her fortune, that many a gentleman would accept into their coffers? Or the fact that she'd been honest with him, had stated that she sought a husband, a love match, and he was found wanting?

He'd told her himself that he wasn't the marrying kind. The fact was not a lie. To be married to him would be on par with torture for a woman wanting a husband who remained faithful and adoring. Abe would never be either of those things. He ran a gambling den for crying out loud. A place where men came to escape their wives and duty to gamble and if they so chose, where they could bring their Cyprians and make use of his private suites upstairs.

"You do." Duncannon's words sounded astonished. Abe could understand that. He himself was feeling oddly out of sorts and not at all comfortable. "Well, well, well. This is a state that I had not thought would occur."

Abe wrenched at his cravat, annoyed at the stifling knot about his neck. "Don't be ridiculous."

"Willow seems quite taken with Lord Herbert. If my summarizations are correct, I suppose you'll have no issue with him courting her. He stated as much last evening when I was playing billiards. I do believe he intends to make her his wife."

A cold shiver raced down Abe's spine, and he started toward the stables, needing to be atop a horse and soon. Away from his insightful friend who was too loose with his opinions. A woman, Miss Perry…Willow…did not kiss him the way that she did and then turn about and marry someone else. The woman could not be so fickle, surely, unless she'd grown to like Lord Perfect. The idea repulsed him to his core.

"She can do whatever she likes," he threw over his shoulder, needing distance before he struck out and punched something, namely his friend's jaw for speaking the truth. Or at least speaking the truth to him and making him see the fact that he did not want to admit.

That Miss Willow Perry had wormed her way under his skin, and no matter how much he may try and remove her, she would not shift.

~

*W*illow strolled with Lord Herbert, his never-ending discourse regarding his home had been sweet and interesting at first, but after an hour of it, she had started to lose enthusiasm for the subject. She glanced about the gardens, spying Lord Ryley and Duncannon striding toward the stables. Duncannon seemed to have stopped Ryley, pulling him about to talk to him. She narrowed her eyes on the pair. Were they arguing?

Lord Ryley glanced in her direction, the disgust that formed on his features telling her all that she needed to know about the gentleman. It had been a mistake that she had kissed him, allowed him such liberties. Even if the memory of his mouth, hot and wet sliding over her breast settled an ache deep down in her core. He was a cad. She'd known it from the first, and it was her fault that she'd allowed herself to be swept up in his arms.

For all his help with her investments, there would not be a repeat of what had occurred between them. No more kisses. No more touches.

She glanced up at Lord Herbert as he spoke of his mother and how much he looked forward to their meeting. Willow smiled and tried to take an interest, but she'd heard the countess wasn't a woman to cross. A lady who had, on many occasions, harangued those she thought required instruction on better manners or decorum.

"We will be returning to town in two days. I look forward to introducing you to her."

If only she felt the same. Willow kept her smile in place, not letting it slip even though the thought of meeting Lady Herbert made her stomach churn. "I've heard of the countess. I look forward to meeting her too. I hope we can be friends."

Lord Herbert patted her hand, and Willow ground her teeth at the condescending way in which he did so. "Never fear, my dear. She will like you very much. You are her friend's niece, after all."

Would like her money she supposed, more than she would like Willow for herself. She had no title. Her aunt had married well, but none of her family on either side of her parents' line had. The countess would not like that no matter how much Lord Herbert may wish it so.

"I intend to head back to London the day after tomorrow. The Duke of Carlisle's ball is the next day, and I do not wish to miss it. It's rumored to be the ball of the season."

"Ah, yes," he said, nodding. "If you will, may I escort you back to London? I shall ride beside the carriage and ensure no harm befalls you and Miss Milton or Miss Clare."

She inwardly sighed. Vexed that she'd allowed Lord Ryley's opinion of Lord Herbert to taint him. He was sweet, caring, and was trying very hard to court her as a gentleman should. Not ravish her beside a running stream and then do everything in his power to avoid her since.

Willow needed to gain her sensibilities back. She would not lose her head to a gentleman who in no way wanted a wife and did not want her. "That is very kind of you, my lord. I would like that very much."

He pulled them to a stop, taking her hand from his arm and kissing her gloved fingers. His eyes held hers as his lips touched her skin. Willow attempted to appear flattered, but she wasn't sure if she succeeded. This was wrong. She knew it to her very center. Being with Lord Herbert did not fire any emotions within her at all. He was kind, could be a friend, but the word bland fluttered throughout her mind whenever they were together.

A marriage to him would be safe. Would give her the protection of his name and enable her to have children. Something she had longed for, for quite some time. She wished, oh how she wanted her blood to heat with every look from his lordship. For every touch or softly spoken word to make her shiver in awareness. But it did not.

Was it because she had not kissed the gentleman? Lord Herbert placed her hand onto his arm, and she realized he'd finished his little gesture and was escorting her back indoors. So lost in her own thoughts she'd not noticed. Hadn't reacted at all. The first time she'd seen Lord Ryley, without even having his dark, wicked gaze on her, she'd known of his presence. Had felt it like a physical caress.

Now, after she'd kissed the gentleman, she was even more aware of him. She frowned, knowing there was only one thing that she could do to remedy the situation. She needed to kiss Lord Herbert and see if, by kissing him, her reaction to him changed. After all, before Lord Ryley she'd not kissed anyone. Mayhap it was due to her lack of awareness and knowledge of men that stopped her from knowing if she could be with someone as their wife. It was possible that after kissing Lord Herbert that her body would become aware of him.

Her skin prickled, and at the terrace doors, she glanced over her shoulder and spied Lord Ryley pushing his mount out across the fields of the estate, his coattails sailing behind him, his dark, wild hair easy to spy amongst the green landscape and, damn it all to hell, her heart skipped a beat.

CHAPTER 11

*A*be lounged on a window seat in the long portrait gallery in the Duke of Whitstone's new estate and stared out onto the manicured grounds below. His melancholy mood was unlike him, and he loathed that he'd been brought low by a woman. Or at least, one particular woman who had continued to stroll about the house with Lord Perfect as if he were the best thing that had ever happened to London in its thousand-year history.

That the bastard threw amused, cocky glances his way, practically rubbing his courtship of Miss Perry in his face wasn't to be borne. If the man did not stop, Abe would have to take the situation into his own hands. Namely, he'd punch the bastard fair on his aristocratic uppity nose.

Thankfully the window nook that he sat within shielded him from anyone else who thought to take in the gallery. Not that the duke and duchess had time as yet to update the images to those of their family members. The estate had been owned by the Earl of Glenmere, a family that had fallen on hard times and had lost their fortune. If he knew his friends at all, they were likely looking after the family portraits to eventually hand them back when they were able to procure them.

A lilting feminine chuckle caught his attention, and he stilled when he recognized it as that of Miss Perry. The deeper tone, however, eluded him, and he pulled the curtain aside a little and glanced down the gallery to see Lord Perfect standing before a large painting of a gentleman with his wolfhound at his feet.

Miss Perry, her profile as ideal as he remembered it, slammed into him like a physical blow, and he clasped the seat he sat upon to stop himself from joining the couple and putting an end to the little tête-à-tête they were hosting.

His lip curled at the image they made. That they looked like a perfect London pair did little to ease his temper. But what he saw next made his blood run cold. Lord Perfect, after he made her chuckle at something he said, leaned down and kissed her.

Not just a quick, sweet kiss either, but one where he drew her up against him and took her mouth like a man who wanted a woman in his bed. Abe stood, fighting the urge to break through their secret interlude. To pummel the basted to a pulp and wrench Miss Perry away from the one man who Abe would never allow her to marry.

He turned toward the window, fisting his hands at his sides, fighting for control. He would not interrupt. If Lord Perfect was the man she wanted, what was it to him? He was going to ruin her anyway. Make her pay for her aunt's wrongdoings. That she was possibly days away from being betrothed to Lord Perfect was indeed ideal. He could take them both down together, and much more easily as a couple. His contacts in London, his business dealings, could make it hard for Lord Perfect financially. The man, so like so many others, was not as perfect as they led everyone to believe, and he had vowels that Abe could purchase.

Thoughts and plans ran through his mind on how to ruin them both. Anger beat through his veins like an elixir of revenge. A gasp sounded behind him, and he jumped as a warm, well-rounded body slammed into his back.

He turned fast enough to clasp Miss Perry's arms and steady her before she tumbled onto her ass. He should let her go, to fall on her backside. It was the least she deserved after kissing the bastard Lord Perfect.

"Lord Ryley." She gulped, her cheeks a bright, splotchy pink as if she'd been caught doing something naughty, which she had.

"Miss Perry," he said, as blandly as he could. He stepped back, putting space between them. He didn't need another reminder of what her body felt like beneath his hands. He knew very well how delicious her curves were. How much he longed to have her in his arms once again so he could savor every ounce of her. "What are you running away from?" he asked, stepping past her and seeing the portrait gallery empty of the Lord Perfect.

"Nothing," she said on a rush, the blush on her cheeks reddening further. Not that he thought it was possible for her to look any more embarrassed, but there you go, she could. Her eyes darted about like a frightened deer, and he raised his brow.

"I thought I saw you before. Just outside in the portrait gallery and quite busy with a certain lord. Are you sure you're not running away?"

She bit her lip, and Abe stilled. Damn it. He wanted to kiss her. To kiss her so deep and long so she would have no other choice but to forget the pompous fool who dared to take such liberties with her.

"You were spying on me?"

He chuckled, seating himself back down. Abe kept watch of her, hoping she wouldn't flee. As much as he loathed himself for it, he longed for her company. Enjoyed their sparring and their kisses—when she wasn't handing them out to anyone else that was.

"Not spying, simply at the right place at a most opportune time." He crossed his legs, clasping his knee with his hands. "I am curious, though. Do you always go about house parties determined on kissing every gentleman that you speak to? First me, and now Lord Perfect. Does his lordship know that you've shared your delights with me as well?"

She crossed her arms at her front, accentuating her breasts in her pretty, green-silk gown. Abe inwardly groaned. Maybe it wasn't such a good idea that she was hidden away in here with him. Not after days of not being near her, not having the delight of teasing the little minx.

"Sounds like spying to me. You ought to be ashamed of yourself."

"Me?" he said, pointing at himself for effect. "I ought to be ashamed of myself? I'm not the one kissing random gentlemen guests with little heed to anyone who could pass you by or come upon you. I heard you and while I should have made my presence known I figured I was here first and so did not. You see," he said, glancing at the book at his side that he'd not opened the whole time he'd been sitting in the window alcove. "I was reading and then rudely interrupted with declarations of intent and disgusting sounds of a pompous fool kissing a woman that he is not worthy of."

Miss Perry gasped, staring at him, and Abe stilled, realizing that he'd said too much. May have given too much away as to what seeing her with Lord Perfect did to him. Drove him to distraction where he wanted to harm the cad physically.

"If you must know, Lord Herbert is courting me. He's going to introduce me to his mother when we return to town. He's escorting me tomorrow, in fact."

Abe stood, having not known that the bastard was escorting her or that she was going home. Both tidbits of information sending his wits spiraling. "You're leaving? But I thought the house party was to continue up to Sunday. Are you so eager to rush back to town to meet his lordship's mother? I know I would not be."

"No? You do not like her, my lord? If I'm not to meet his lordship's mother, then maybe you'd like me to meet yours. You do seem so very put out that his lordship is courting me. Are you by any chance, Lord Ryley, jealous?" she said, leaning toward him and leaving not a whisper of space between their mouths.

That hers twisted into a knowing smirk snapped the little amount of control that he'd been holding on to. He wrenched her into his arms. She gasped, and he found himself watching her, realizing with some delight that the wench was enjoying his manhandling of her. His inability not to react to her taunting him with ideals and dreams of marrying another pleased her.

Abe wasn't sure if he liked that realization or not and didn't bother trying to determine the outcome of that thought when he took her lips in a searing kiss, eliminating all thoughts entirely.

*T*his. This was what it was like to be kissed by a man who knew how to do it right. Willow stood on tiptoes and kissed Lord Ryley back with as much enthusiasm and ability as she could remember from their last embrace.

He tasted of sweet tea and roguery, his wavy, dark locks in her fingers soft and supple in her hands. She dragged him down to her mouth, again and again, and she reveled in the feel of his tongue tangling with hers. Oh yes, this kiss was so much more than the one she had shared with Lord Perfect.

His had been closed-mouthed, stilted as if he was unsure if he could merely peck her lips or kiss her as Lord Ryley was now kissing her. Her back came up against the small partitioned wall between the windows, and he pinned her there. His hard, muscular chest teasing her nipples to hardened peaks. His large, strong hands slid down her back, eliciting a shiver down her spine before one hand clasped her bottom, pulling her hard against him.

Willow gasped, his straining manhood positioned at her aching core, and without thought, she moved against him. Sliding her sex against his, the annoyance of clothing, the muffled sensation making her impatient.

There were too many clothes between them. She wanted to feel him. To let him show her how it should be between a man and a woman. Between a husband and wife.

A moan rent the air, and she realized it was her as his hand slipped around her bottom to skim near the opening of her pantalettes. The burning need, the delicious ache between her thighs demanded soothing, to be stroked.

"You're wet for me, Willow." He kissed his way down

her throat, taking little bites against her shoulder. "You know what that means, do you not?"

She shook her head, mumbling an incoherent answer that even she didn't understand. Not that she understood much at the moment. This was all wrong. He was wrong for her, even if he did feel so very right at the moment. Lord Ryley, the Spanish Scoundrel, would never marry anyone she was sure, indeed, not her. She wasn't connected enough, or wild enough for his lordship. From what she knew of him, of where he spent most of his time—In his gambling den—he lived hard and fast.

It was not what she wanted. She wanted to live, yes, but she wanted a family, a marriage of the truest sense. A life that would suit her. Lord Ryley did not suit at all.

She remembered his question. "No," she managed, sucking in a breath as his fingers skimmed her opening.

"It means that you like my touch. I'd wager you did not get as hot and wet when that popinjay Lord Perfect kissed you."

The reminder that she'd kissed two men in a matter of minutes slammed into Willow, and she shoved him away. He stumbled back, but where she thought to see smug understanding, she only saw a burning need in his eyes that matched hers. How could a man so unlike what she wanted make her feel so much that she would forget all propriety and damn it, Lord Herbert as well?

Willow took a calming breath, reaching up to check her hair and thankfully finding the pins in place. She couldn't keep allowing such liberties. Nor could she keep wanting to have them. If she were serious about finding a husband, she could not be ruined by the most infamous rake in London.

"No more," she said, holding up her hand when he

went to step toward her. "We cannot keep doing this. Whatever this is," she said, gesturing between them.

"You like my kisses and my touch. Why stop when you do not have to?" He watched her, and she could tell he was trying to figure out what to do. What to say. There was little he could do or say that could help this situation. She needed to return to London if only to get away from the man before her.

As much as she may wish it, deep down in her soul, she knew that he could not be changed. Men like Lord Ryley did not fall in love and be loyal to their wives. She was deluding her hopes to think otherwise. Lord Ryley had spent far too many years disillusioned by the *ton* and having too much fun snubbing his nose at their rules of propriety. His opinion on marriage wasn't much better.

"I will not sleep with you, my lord."

"Abe, please."

She swallowed, having not thought he would give her leave to use his name. Not after denying him what he wanted.

Her.

A shiver raked her skin, and she rubbed her arms, chilled all of a sudden. "I cannot call you that." Not that she didn't wish to call him by his name, but it was too personal. Too intimate. Not as intimate as what they just partook in, but still, it was his given name.

"Yes you can. I want you to." He reached out, taking her hand and idly playing with her fingers. "We do not have to sleep together for me to give you pleasure." He flicked open the two pearl buttons at her wrist and slipped her glove free. Lifting her hand, he brought it to his mouth, kissing her palm. His hot kiss was similar to his kisses on her mouth, and she trembled, wondering what he would do after such a statement.

"So I'll remain a virgin?" she breathed, biting her lip to stop herself from stepping against him and forgetting all her own rules and dreams and giving herself over to the Spanish Scoundrel.

He grinned knowingly, and she wished she knew what he was thinking. She was not going to give herself to this man. Not without a proposal of marriage, and that most definitely was not going to happen.

"Yes, and let me show you how."

The pressure of his hold on her hand increased, and she knew he was a moment from pulling her against him again. Should he do so, she would not be able to resist. Not a second time. It had taken all her force of will to push him away when all she wanted was whatever he was willing to give her. No matter the consequences.

Willow wrenched her hand free, picked up her glove and left him staring at her, his eyes wide as she started down the picture gallery hall, determined to make her room without being ruined by a rake. Debauched in a window alcove by Marquess Ryley.

His chuckle followed her, and she strode faster. "See you back in London, Willow."

She cringed, hating that the sound of her name on his lips was like an elixir that she wanted beyond anything else. Even a perfect, safe marriage with a man like Lord Herbert.

CHAPTER 12

*T*he London season was in full swing by the time they arrived back in town. Willow attended the Duke of Carlisle's ball, and every night since had attended one or another event. The opera, a night at Covent Garden, numerous balls and dinners. All of them pleasant, and all of them leaving her irritated and frustrated when they came to an end.

Stupid fool that she was, she'd thought when Lord Ryley had said he would see her in London that he'd seek her out. He had not. In fact, she'd not seen him at all.

Which was the sole reason she was now in a Hackney carriage and on her way to Hell's Gate. Without the chaperonage of her friends, who were at an event with the Duchess of Whitstone.

If her friends found out she'd played them by feigning a headache to stay home, they would never forgive her. But she had to know. She had to see if Lord Ryley was back in London and quite settled in, not seeking her out. If that were the case, then she could continue on her path with Lord Herbert. It would prove to her beyond any doubt that his lordship was the gentleman for her and not some scoundrel who played with women and then left them to pick up their scattered hearts afterward.

Willow scoffed. What was she saying? She wasn't heartbroken. Not at all. Lord Ryley had been a pleasurable experience, that was for certain, but that was all. She had not given her heart to him. A silly notion she would not entertain again.

She checked over her outfit, men's breeches, knee-high boots. The waistcoat and superfine coat fitted her to perfection that she'd had her modiste sew up for her. She didn't want him to recognize her tonight, and with a new wig of short-cropped black hair, Willow didn't think he would.

Arriving at the club, she paid the driver to wait and went inside. The sound of music met her ears, and a small group of musicians were set up in one corner, playing while the gathered gentlemen gambled. Very few paid her attention, too caught up in their card games or the women on their laps.

Willow strode about, looking for the one gentleman who'd occupied her mind far too much over the last few days. Why she couldn't fathom. Lord Herbert had been attentive at all the balls and parties, and she was certain that in a matter of weeks, if not days, he would offer for her.

Not that she'd met his mother yet, but she felt sure to very soon, or so Lord Herbert said.

Standing at the foot of the stairs, Willow bowed to a woman who walked past, eyeing her in the fashion rakes glanced at the fairer sex. After being kissed by Lord Ryley, Willow understood what the woman walking by wanted from any gentleman willing to pay her fee.

Lord Ryley's office was up on the second level, and she turned, climbing the stairs. If she found him here, then at least she would know what he was about. What had kept him from seeking her out about town.

A couple ran past her, giggling and fondling each other before disappearing into a room and closing the door with a decided slam. Willow edged her way along the passageway, making sure to look like she was taking an interest in the gaming below stairs.

She stopped where the door she believed led into Lord Ryley's office was and leaned on the railing. The door was closed, and she frowned. She couldn't open it and glance inside, he would surely know who she was if she did that, but she could wait and hope that he'd come out.

A sultry laugh caught her attention, and she glanced toward the staircase, spying the same woman that Lord Ryley deemed his mistress.

Her long, dark locks flowed about her back unbound. Her lips painted a deep, glossy red, and she oozed sensuality. Willow sucked in a breath as the woman ran a finger along a gentleman that she passed before winking at him. Her gown was transparent and left nothing to the imagination.

Willow turned, staring downstairs as Abe's mistress knocked on the door behind her, before entering.

Thankfully she left the door open, and Willow shifted up the corridor a little to be out of sight, but within hearing.

"Darling, come downstairs and dance with me. It's not every night that we have musicians playing."

"Not tonight, Lottie."

Willow bit her lip at the grave, distracted voice of Lord Ryley. She heard a pouty sigh from the woman. Her

117

stomach curdled at the idea that a woman as beautiful, as sinful as the Spanish Scoundrel, was the woman who shared his bed.

Despair tore through her. With a mistress as seductive as that woman was, it wasn't any wonder he'd not sought her out. She wasn't as worldly, or as beautiful, and it was only stupidity on her behalf that a small part of her had hoped that he'd change for her. That he'd fall madly in love with her and leave all this debauchery behind.

Willow glanced over her shoulder and, through the door, spied a mirror across the room. It gave her a direct view of Lord Ryley seated at his desk. He was bent over a stack of papers, his hair askew as if he'd run his hand through it too many times. The woman glided about the room, her flowing red gown doing nothing to pull his lordship's gaze.

A little part of her liked that he ignored the siren. At least she didn't have to be privy to his ogling his lover.

"Ever since you returned to town, you've been a bore." The woman rounded on him, coming to a halt before his desk. "Do you not want me anymore, Abe?" she purred, running a hand across the low cut of her dress. Lord Ryley. *Abe*…did look up then, a flicker of appreciation burning in his opaque orbs.

Willow blinked back the prick of tears at seeing him look at his lover with renewed interest. Damn him and his treatment of her. He was as bad as the *ton* termed him. Scoundrel fitted his character to a fault.

"You know I'm simply catching up on work, Lottie. No need to be jealous over what keeps you in the luxurious life you now live."

The woman's pout should be on the stage, not just for Lord Ryley's eyes. His lover sauntered around the table, coming to sit on the desk before him, scattering his papers. Lord Ryley leaned back in his chair, watching her keenly.

"Perhaps you'd like to have a little repast, my lord?" she said, spreading her legs and sliding her wine-red gown up to pool at her waist.

Willow felt her mouth gape, and she fought to catch her breath. He grinned, wickedly, as the word *bastard* reverberated around in her mind. She had come here tonight to see if he was simply distracted, and distracted he most certainly was, among other things. Namely, his mistress.

The sniffing he did about Willow's skirts in Hampton was merely amusement for him. She shook her head. She was a fool. Had been fooled. It was her fault. His reputation had preceded him, and she'd allowed his wicked kisses and ardent touch to sway her into allowing him liberties she should not have.

He would never change. His actions right now in his office with his mistress told her that, and she would not waste a moment longer wondering if he'd ever see the value in her, want to change for love. He didn't love her. He'd loved no one but himself.

Willow turned and glanced down at the gamblers, many of whom she knew, most of them married or betrothed. There were few who didn't have their mistresses with them. What was she doing here? This was not the life she wanted. No matter how much she may have enjoyed his lordship's touch. She had allowed herself to be caught up in his seductive game, but never again. Lord Herbert was kind, yes, a little boring perhaps, but he would be true to her at least. With a marriage such as the one that loomed before her with his lordship, Willow believed love could bloom. If nurtured in time, it would grow and thrive.

Lord Ryley's deep chuckle sounded in the room behind

her, and she glanced through the door, not bothering to try to hide the fact she was watching them. His mistress was on his lap now, his arms loosely holding her about her waist.

Her feet would not move, no matter how much she didn't want to see what she was witnessing. Lord Ryley glanced over his mistress's shoulder and spied her. His smile slipped before he stood, causing his lover to fall on the floor before him.

"Willow," he said, striding around the desk.

Willow fled down the hall, heedless of the fact that she was the only one running out of this cesspit of rakes and bastards all. The sound of his Cyprian's protestations on being dumped on the floor floated to her ears. A small crow of pleasure ran through her that the woman had been dumped on her behind.

Not that any of this was the mistress's fault. Willow allowing Lord Ryley liberties was all on her. She'd let him play her the fool, and now she would have to live with that consequence. Or at least her fickle, stupid heart would.

"Willow. Stop."

She didn't halt, her small frame making it easier for her to weave her way through the crowd. A few gentlemen took an interest, laughing and ribbing Lord Ryley at having not known his interest lay with the same sex.

Willow ignored them all. Her course to reach the carriage outside and to run headlong into a marriage with Lord Herbert her goal. She made the doors, throwing them open and running full pelt toward the carriage. She could hear Lord Ryley's footsteps hard on her heels, but she wouldn't stop. She had to make the carriage. Had to get away.

Strong, immovable arms wrapped about her waist and

hauled her to a stop. The feel of his chest, hard up against her back, sent a frustrating thrill down her spine, and she kicked at his shins as best she could, trying to remove herself from his hold.

"Get your hands off me, you rutting bastard." He stilled behind her and she did too. She'd never used such vulgar words before, but having said them aloud and to this very gentleman, in particular, was liberating. He deserved to be called out for what he was. How dare he play with her with so little regard? He knew she was inno-cent in the ways of men, and yet, still, he teased and taunted her with the possibility of more.

Even though she'd been a fool to silently hope, wonder if such a man could be changed by love. Lord Ryley was not that man.

"Tsk. Tsk. Tsk, my little hellcat. What has all your bris-tles upright?"

Willow wrenched free, rounding on him. She started at his closeness and gritted her teeth at having to look up to meet his gaze. The heat she read there did odd things to her insides, and she narrowed her eyes, reminding herself as to why she'd fled from his gaming hell in the first place.

"You, Lord Ryley. You and the way you treat women."

"Really?" he asked, crossing his arms, the action making her aware of his muscular frame and the fact he wasn't wearing a coat, only a shirt. Her gaze flicked to his neck, noting that too was without a cravat. He was half-undressed, and the awareness wasn't helpful.

"Yes. Really. You played with me in Hampton. Admit that you did. And now back in London, I'm to be tossed to the curb like all your past lovers." Why was she saying such things? She didn't care that he'd moved on. This was a good outcome for all of them. She was going to marry someone else, and all memory of the man before her would be eliminated from her mind.

The lie almost made her scoff aloud.

Damn him.

"We were never lovers, but seeing you in those breeches again, I can be persuaded to change my mind."

She gasped, stepping back. "You're a cad," she growled. "I would not touch you, not after I just spied you fondling your mistress. She looked more than willing. Why don't you go back upstairs and satisfy her, my lord? I'm not interested." Willow turned on her heel, calling out the direction to the hackney cab driver who turned to face the road, no doubt well absorbed in their public argument as she was.

"Oh, no you don't, Miss Perry," he said, his voice deep and menacing. He followed her into the carriage, rapping on the roof. The vehicle lurched forward and she glared at him. "What do you think you're doing. Get out at once."

He gestured toward the window. "We're moving. It wouldn't be safe, and anyway, we're not finished."

Willow laughed and hoped he heard the sarcasm in her gesture. "Oh no, we're finished, my lord. Not that we ever started." Which wasn't entirely true, but still, if he hoped for more fondling, more kisses, he would be mistaken. She'd spit in his eye before she did that again.

"Are you jealous of my mistress?" he queried as if he'd simply asked her about the weather.

She stared at him, anger spiking through her blood. "Jealous? No, but your actions confirmed to me what I already knew of you. I should have listened to everyone and kept away from you. I'll not be fooled a second time."

His jaw tightened, and he glanced away a moment. "Lottie is no longer my mistress, no matter how much she wishes to be. When I returned to town after the house party, I paid her enough to be comfortable for however long she wishes not to have a protector. Lottie is a playful woman and up for teasing if it means she gets what she wants."

Willow scoffed, leaning forward. "And she would have had you had I not interrupted?" Lord Ryley leaned forward, their breaths intermingling.

"She would not have had me, damn it."

"You lie, my lord."

"I do not lie, Miss Perry."

"Really? And I'm to believe that?" she asked, arching her brow.

"Yes, you should, because the only woman whom I've wanted lately is the little minx sitting across from me now."

~

illow's eyes widened before they narrowed, her distrust of him evident. His words slammed into him like a body punch, and he accepted them for the truth that they were. He did want Willow. Wanted her more than he'd ever desired anyone in his life up to this point.

She was everything he didn't need. A woman looking for love, a family, a secure, peaceful future. Where his life was chaos. Endless nights of debauchery, days of gambling, and endless idleness. All things he'd enjoyed up to the point he had met her. Now she'd thrown his life into turmoil.

He didn't want a wife. The thought repulsed him, but the idea of Willow marrying Lord Perfect, hell, anyone for that matter, repulsed him more. He'd never allow such an outcome. If she married, he'd lose her forever. Not that he'd won her at all. Even after all their kisses, their times together, she was prickly and distrustful.

Rightfully so since he'd embarked on making her pay for her family's part in his mother's fall from society's grace.

"I don't believe you," she said. Her eyes stole to his lips, and heat tickled down his spine.

"Believe this, then." He wrenched her onto his lap, taking her lips in a searing kiss that rocked his axis off-balance. Kissing her was all he wanted to do, feel her sweet curves in his hands again as her mouth battled with his.

He growled as her tongue slipped against his own, and he clasped her nape, holding her to him, not ever wanting to let go. Their hands were everywhere, her little gasps as he explored her every curve, her lovely full breasts that were a perfect handful.

Abe had to feel her, satisfy his doubts that she wanted him as much as he wanted her. He wrenched her front falls open, reaching into her breeches and finding her deliciously wet. She moaned, kissing him deeper. The kiss turned scalding, their mouths fused, their tongues exploring, demanding more from the other.

He couldn't get enough. Would never have enough of her. "Damn it, Willow. You drive me to distraction."

Her fingers slid down his chest, his heart beating a continuous thrum of need. She shifted on his lap, straddling him, and for the second time this night, his world moved beneath his feet. Never before had he ever been on unsolid ground. He was a man who controlled everything, who his friends were, his estate, club, his lovers. But the woman in his arms was everything he disliked of the *ton*, his enemy, and yet, he could not let her go. Would not let her go, no matter how much he should.

She was so wet, her moisture coating his fingers and telling him that she wanted him as much as he wanted her. Even if she protested to his face that he was a cad. An ass. All true, but damn it, this right now, Willow in his arms felt right. Made him forget his past, forget all the wrongs done to his family until all he was left with was satisfying her. Making her happy.

"Oh yes," she gasped against his mouth. His cock strained against his breeches, and he cursed the fact she was wearing men's clothing. He wanted her. Wanted to fuck her, here and now, their location be damned.

"Tell me what you want, Willow." He would not force her, but a small part of him hoped she'd allow him to have her. To claim her as his.

"Just this. What you're doing now." Her plea, her eyes sleepy with unsated desire pulled at something in his chest, and he could not refuse her anything. He slid against her folds, sliding into her hot core with one finger while his thumb rolled against her bud of pleasure.

Her gasp, her undulating body against his hand, made his cock ache for release. He wanted her with a frenzy unusual for him. He wanted to satisfy her, show her all that could be between them. He cared...

Abe inwardly swore, knowing what she made him feel was the truth of his situation. He cared for the woman in his arms. That was what the difference was between her and his past bedmates. He wanted to make her happy, satisfied, and not just in a sexual way. He wanted to hear her laugh, see her more than just at balls and parties.

With his free hand, he pulled at her breeches, giving him more access to her. She tasted of vice, and his mouth watered with the thought of kissing where his hand worked her sex. Her kisses against his lips became frenzied and deep.

Abe took all that she was willing to give him. Her excitement slid over his fingers as he worked her, teased her swollen bud until, at last, she cried out against his mouth. She fucked his hand, although he knew she didn't know that was what she was doing.

Need roared through him, overwhelming and urgent. He wanted her. Wanted to lay her down on the seat across from them, rip her breeches free and sheathe himself deep into her aching core. He worked her until the last of her climax ebbed from her body. She slumped against him, her head limp upon his shoulder.

Abe freed his hand, adjusting her breeches as best he could before wrapping his arms about her. He wasn't the type of man to cuddle after any sexual interchange, but with Willow, it was different. She made him want to hold her. To ensure she was satisfied and to let her know she was safe.

A sense of wellbeing, of calm, settled over him, and he placed a quick kiss to her temple, the sweet, berry scent of her hair making him grin. He held her close, rubbing her back as she regained her breath, content to stay like this always.

He frowned into the darkened carriage as they rolled through the streets of London. Who would have guessed that the one woman he'd sworn revenge on was the first woman who had captured his heart?

And he cared about her more than anything else, even seeking retribution for his mother.

CHAPTER 13

The following afternoon Willow sat in her private parlor and flipped through the latest designs from the *La Belle Assemblee*. She had ordered tea and biscuits, but she could not concentrate on the women's fashion magazine. It was pointless. That Lord Ryley was going to be calling on her to go over the investments as per their arrangement last evening after he'd dropped her home, made concentration impossible.

He'd kissed her so deeply, so passionately before opening the carriage door that she'd almost stumbled up the stairs to the front of her house. It was silly of her. The man was not looking for a wife, but dear heavens, what he'd made her feel last evening was nothing like she'd ever undergone before in her life.

She experienced a taste of the pleasure his talented hands could bring forth in her at Hampton, but that had been nothing compared to last night. The satisfaction had been searing, consuming, and left her wanting more, not less.

His hand upon her had brought her such pleasure that

to remember it now made her stomach clench deliciously. She wanted him, and this afternoon she would seduce him. Here. In her private parlor while her friends were out for the afternoon with Hallie.

It was scandalous behavior, and she was taking a great risk in wanting him in this way, but she could not help herself. If she could not have him as a husband, she would have him in this way before she married a man who would love her back.

A light knock on the door sounded, and her butler introduced Marquess Ryley, a small line of disapproval on her old retainer's forehead. Willow thanked the servant. "Close the door please, Thomas. I'm discussing business and do not wish to be disturbed."

Lord Ryley glanced at her, brows raised, and she walked past him as her butler closed the door. She snipped the lock and turned to face Abe, but he was already upon her. He seized her in his arms, walking her back until she came up against the door. His heat, his delicious self, pressed into her, and her body yearned for him. For more of what he'd given her a taste of yesterday.

"I've missed you," he said, kissing her soundly, his tongue tangling with hers. Willow clutched at him, her body a riot of needs and wants. Of hopes and dreams.

"Me too." She slid her hand over his chest, taking her time in learning every flexed, sinewy muscle that moved under her palm. Willow slipped her hands beneath his coat, pushing it off his shoulders to fall at their feet.

He met her gaze, a wicked light in his eyes as she made quick work of the buttons on his silver waistcoat. That too, slipped from his shoulders to pool on the floor.

"Am I the only one who's going to be naked here this morning, Miss Perry?"

"Willow, please." She threw him a mischievous glance. "And no, you're not. I'm simply quicker at undressing you than you are me."

"Is that so?" His deep baritone held a warning that she wanted to poke. To see how far she could push him before he snapped. Before he showed her why it was that he was called a scoundrel.

"I'm winning so far," she said flippantly.

He drew her close, making short work of the small clips down her back. Her gown whooshed to the floor, and then her shift too was lifted over her head, leaving her with nothing but her stockings on.

The urge to cover herself ran through her, but glancing up and seeing the admiration, the heat in Abe's gaze stilled her hands at her sides. She raised her chin, watching him. Her skin prickled into goose bumps as he took in her form, admiringly.

He reached out, running a finger across one breast, circling her nipple, making it pebble into puckered flesh. She bit her lip, her breathing ragged. This is what it was like to be seduced. And by someone who knew how and she would enjoy every moment of it. If this was to be her only chance with a man other than her husband, at least it would be with one of London's most renowned rakes.

~

*A*be swallowed as he took in the sweet, shivering form of Willow before him. He'd come here today to go through the investments he'd propositioned her with. Investments which he was going to deny her now. He could not do it to her. Hurt her financially. Not because she was giving herself to him, but because she did not deserve it.

She may be the niece of the woman who ruined his mother's place in London society, but she was innocent of any crimes against his family.

Now that she was here, his to claim, he knew there was only one outcome that would suit him now. Willow had to marry him. Had to be his wife. It was unimaginable the thought of seeing her as someone else's wife, and so it was the only course open to them.

She was the only woman he'd ever cared about. Thought and planned for. While it may not be love, what he felt, his affection for her was profound and more than he'd ever felt with anyone else.

He stepped closer to her, pushing her against the door and ravaged her puckered nipple with his tongue. Her gasp and rapid breaths told him she was hot, wet, and ready for him. The thought of sinking deep into her hot core sent a bolt of lust to his groin, and he nipped her breast in punishment of leaving him so hard.

Her fingers spiked into his hair, holding him to her, and he moved over to her other breast, reveling in the ample heaviness of her breasts. "So damn sweet," he said, kissing down her stomach, circling her navel before dropping to his knees.

He glanced up the length of her, caught her lust-filled gaze as he slowly kissed his way toward her glistening mons.

"What are you doing?" she breathed, her fingers massaging his scalp and sending a shiver of bliss down his spine.

"I'm going to kiss you here."

"Where?" she squeaked, holding him away from her.

He chuckled, reached out and slipped his finger over her bud, past her folds to tease her core. "Right here, love."

∽

*W*illow watched, entranced as Abe kissed her in the one spot she'd never thought anyone would ever go. Not with their mouth at least. She marveled at the sight of him as his tongue flicked out, teasing her at the same spot his hand had teased her in the carriage the day before.

Without thought, she lifted one leg and slipped it over his shoulder.

"That's it, love. Open for me."

She bit her lip, leaning back on the door as his tongue flicked and teased, his lips kissing her most private of parts. Heat coursed through her, a sweet ache settled at her core, and she wanted him to kiss her there. To run his clever fingers against her opening.

And then his mouth was there too, kissing, laving, teasing her to the point that she'd not thought possible to stand. She moaned and quickly bit her lip from making too much noise. They were at the door, after all. The servants could be standing on the other side.

He suckled on her, and a bolt of pleasure spiked through her. She clasped his hair, undulating against his mouth. All thoughts of propriety vanished. All that was left was the exquisite gratification coursing through her.

"Oh yes, Abe," she gasped, not caring how loud her words were.

He growled his approval, the tremor of his voice sending another bolt of heat to her sex. She could feel it again, a building up to the pinnacle of climax that she'd had yesterday. This time though, it was stronger, more carnal as his mouth worked her to a frenzy.

She moved on him, ground her body against his

wicked tongue, and then his hand slid against her folds, his finger delving deep into her body. Willow clasped his shoulders as tremor after tremor ran through her core, spiraling up to burst through her body.

Bliss. Pure bliss.

And then she was in his arms. He carried her to the daybed on the other side of the room. Willow made short work of his breeches, ripping his front falls open and not waiting for him to slip them down before they tumbled onto the soft, cushioned bed.

She wrapped her legs about his waist, rubbing her throbbing sex against his phallus It was deliciously hard, shooting more tremors through her each time he thrust against her.

"Are you sure, Willow?" he asked, reaching down between them. "There is no going back from here."

"Please. I need you," she said, placing him at her core.

"Damn it. I can't deny you anything." He gave one sharp thrust and took her. She stilled as a stinging pain ripped at her core, and she cringed, having not thought it would hurt so much.

"I'm sorry," he gasped, kissing her deep and long. His tongue, the slow ebb of his kiss, took her mind off the fullness of him, the little slice of pain she'd just endured. And then he started to move, a slight rock to begin as she became used to his invasion of her body.

The pain ebbed away and she was left with only a fulfilling ache that begged to be sated. Willow clutched him, unable to get enough, get close enough to the pleasure he promised. Their bodies joined in a dance of desire, his every stroke lighting a fire within her core that sparked and teased her to burn.

Willow arched her back, the abrasive hairs on his chest

teasing her nipples and sending a whole different type of gratification to course through her body.

"I've wanted to fuck you for so long," he gasped against her lips, catching her gaze. They stared at each other while he pumped hard and deep into her core. Willow reached up, clasping his face in her hands. His crude words ought to disgust her, turn her away, and yet if anything, they had the opposite reaction. She loved hearing that he wanted her so much. So much that he dropped his titled mannerisms and became just a man.

Hers…

"I've wanted you too." It was the truth of the situation, and there was little point in denying it. Lord Ryley was not for her, but today, right now, he was all she wanted, and she would take what he would give her. If only this once.

There was no future with the man causing her emotions to riot, her body to clamp and shiver deliciously beneath him. He was wild, and she wanted something tame. Not letting the thought take hold and dampen her emotions, Willow pulled Abe down for a kiss and forgot everything but what he was doing to her. All that he was gifting her with.

Heat spiraled at her core as he rocked faster into her. With each thrust, he teased her deep inside. The urge to beg, to plead for more sat on her tongue, and she threw her head back, gasping for strength to stand any more teasing that he wrought upon her.

"I'm never going to get enough of you," he gasped against her lips.

She kissed him, her heart skipping a beat at his sweet words before pleasure burst bright and strong through her core, shooting out into her limbs, her arms, everywhere. Willow cried out his name and reveled in the sound of hers on his lips as warm liquid spilled onto her stomach.

They slumped together, their breathing ragged. Willow ran a hand down Abe's back, eliciting a shiver. "That, my lord, was simply quite scandalous and marvelous," she sighed, lying back, spent and satisfied beyond imagining. Her legs felt of jelly, her arms weak, her body lethargic as if she could sleep for a week.

He rolled to her side, leaning up on one arm, watching her. His free hand reached out, circling her nipples that were hard buttons of sensation. "I fear, Miss Perry, that what we've done here today must be and will be repeated often. I simply must insist."

She chuckled, glancing at him quickly. "Is that wise, my lord? You said yourself you're not the marrying type, and you know that I'm husband-hunting this season. What if I fall *enceinte*? Will you marry me then?"

He stilled, and she grinned, knowing only too well that he'd not thought that far ahead. That their tryst today would only ever happen once, just as she planned. The only children she would bear would be her husband's, no matter how enjoyable sharing Lord Ryley's bed had been, this rendezvous would only happen once.

She sat up, patting his chest. "We have taken precautions today. Nothing will come of it. You're free to return to the lifestyle you adore so much, and I am free to marry whomever I choose. At least I can thank you for instructing me in the ways of the marriage bed. I must confess that I'm looking forward to married life a lot more now."

134

*a*be gaped at Willow before he realized she was dressing, and he was still lying on the daybed, his breeches halfway down his legs and his cock laying across his leg for anyone to ogle.

He shuffled to the side of the bed, shucking up his breeches and glancing about for his shirt. The thought of Willow increasing with his child had not entered his mind before now, but now that it had the thought of it filled him with pleasure.

A most unwelcome emotion considering he never intended to be a father. Marriages were not an institution he held in high regard, and he would never father a child out of wedlock. Spying his shirt near the door, he strode over to it quickly, slipping it on, along with his waistcoat and jacket.

He turned, fixing his cravat, and his mouth dried at the sight of Willow, attempting to hook the small little tabs at the back of her dress. Warmth speared his chest at the sight of her, sweet and undemanding. She ought to be commanding, telling him that after taking her virginity that he would marry her, make her his wife.

The words that he needed to say to do the right thing lodged in his throat and would not come. She could fall pregnant, be the mother of his child, and still, he couldn't voice the possibility. Instead, he strode over to her, twisted her about, and started to clip together the small ties on the back of her gown.

Never before had he taken the time to stay, to help his lovers dress. He'd always left them where they slept and went about his business. No ties, no emotions. Nothing.

He was a cad through and through. He'd never really thought about it much, but his name, the Spanish

Scoundrel, really did fit him very well. He was certainly acting the scoundrel right now to Willow.

"We shall discuss the investments tomorrow, perhaps. If you're free."

She waved his concern away, turning so he could admire her profile. The sight of her, her beauty, her alabaster skin kissed with the lightest shade of rose after their lovemaking made his stomach clench. Hell, she was a temptress, a woman who made him want to forget all his self-imposed rules and decrees. Made him want to throw them all aside and do whatever the hell made her happy.

"Oh, never mind the investments. I looked over them with my solicitor and we agreed on the Welsh Coal Mine. I've already instructed him to invest some of my funds into the scheme."

Abe stilled, a cold shiver running down his spine. For a moment, his mind worked furiously, and his gut clenched, threatening to cast up his accounts. "How much did you invest?" he managed to ask, hoping it was only a small sum.

"Thirty thousand pounds. I know it's a third of my inheritance, but I trust you and your business acumen." At his silence, she glanced at him over her shoulder. "Is that not enough, you think? Should I have invested more?"

Fuck!

"May I suggest that I visit your solicitor just to ensure that all is in order?" Abe prayed that she'd give him the details of the offices so he could travel down there immediately and stop the transaction. Damn it. He was a bastard for even thinking to do such a thing to her. She was innocent and didn't deserve such treatment.

Panic made his fingers clumsy on her gown, and he took a calming breath, trying to right her dress before leaving. He had to go. Now. If her solicitor was to place her money on the scheme he'd optioned for her, she would lose all that she invested.

"How many more clips do you have to do?" she asked, peeking over her shoulder.

Even with his mind in turmoil, his stomach in his throat, threatening to choke him, her looking back at him, her dark-blue orbs with a teasing light within them made him want to kiss her. To lay her down on the daybed behind them and while away the day making love.

Abe cleared his throat, stepping around her and starting for the door. He was rattled, his mind hazy after one of the best shags of his life.

What was he talking about? One of the best shags? It was the best shag he'd ever had, and she'd been a virgin. The idea of what they could do together when she became more self-aware, more open to other things that they could do made his cock twitch.

"The address?" he queried again, keeping his distance from her lest he pull her into his arms and ravage her a second time. To do so would be unforgivable. She needed time to heal after their afternoon together.

"Oh yes, I have a spare card here on my desk." She walked over to a small lady's portable writing chest, and opening a drawer, pulled out a small card. With a smile on her delectable lips that were a deep shade of pink after their many kisses, she came over to him, handing him the card. "Thank you again for helping me with the investments. I would like more advice, if you're willing, on others if you know of any."

He stared at her, feeling the lowest cad on earth. The Welsh mine looked like a winning investment on paper, and simply because he'd had the documents forged. He threw her a pleased smile that was as wooden as his heart. "My pleasure. I'll call on them directly to ensure all is in order."

Abe leaned down and kissed her, unable to deny himself one last taste of her before he turned and left, shutting the door softly behind him. He kept his calm until he made his carriage, and then he yelled out the direction and for haste.

His driver, sensing the urgency, made short work through the London traffic to Willow's solicitor's offices on Harley street. Within ten minutes, the carriage rocked to a halt before a brown-brick building. Without waiting for his driver, Abe threw open the carriage door and strode as fast as he could without looking like a man on a full run. A gentleman stood at the front wooden counter, looking at him expectantly.

"I'm Marquess Ryley. I need to have an urgent meeting with…with…" He fumbled about in his coat and found the card in his pocket. "Mr. Turner, if you will. It's urgent."

The young man's eyes widened, and he bobbed his head so quickly, Abe feared for his health. "Of course, my lord. Right away, my lord."

Abe cooled his heels only a few moments before a short, stout man with a receding hairline wobbled out into the foyer. "Lord Ryley. It is a pleasure to meet you. Please come to my office."

Abe followed him and sat on the chair across from the older man, who picked up his spectacles and placed them on his nose.

"Now, what is it that I can do for you, my lord?"

Abe cleared his throat, now that he was here he was unsure how to start this conversation without making himself look like an ass. He resigned himself; there was no other way than to tell the solicitor the truth and hope it wasn't too late for Willow.

"A Miss Willow Perry gave me your address as my coming here today is in regard to the investments into the Cornwall coal mine that you're helping her invest in. I have reason to believe the documents were forged, and the returns on the investment were highly exaggerated. If Miss Perry were to invest in the mine, it will, as sure as I'm sitting here, fail, and she will lose the money invested."

Mr. Turner stared at him a moment, his face turning an awful shade of gray. "Are you well, Mr. Turner?" he asked. The last thing he required was for this man to keel over in front of him. Abe needed him to fix the problem that Abe had caused. He shook his head at his absurdity. What had he been thinking! Should Willow find out what he'd done, what he'd planned to do, she would never forgive him. Never trust him. And rightfully so.

"Miss Perry authorized the payment while staying at the Duke and Duchess of Whitstone's estate. The money has been invested."

For a moment, Abe felt as though his body was not his own, that he wasn't sitting before a man, and listening to him tell him that Abe hadn't just lost thirty thousand pounds of Miss Perry's inheritance. He ran a hand over his jaw, at a loss as to what to do.

The realization that his revenge was complete brought no pleasure. A pain seized in the vicinity of his heart, and he clutched his chest. This would hurt Willow, and that, in turn, would hurt him. He cared for her. While he would never forgive Willow's aunt for her treatment of his mother or that of Lord Perfect's parent, nor would he allow what had happened to impact what he'd started to feel for Willow.

Not that it mattered what he felt for her any longer for this would crush her. She would hate him. *Fuck it!* He took a calming breath when his vision swam.

He would not faint like a matron seeing her charge kiss a rogue. He had to fix this. Somehow, he would fix this.

"You must put a stop on the payment. The investment is not sound."

Mr. Turner frowned at Abe before he turned to his desk, shuffling through papers scattered atop it. "But I have a letter here from Miss Perry stating that you, Lord Ryley endorsed this particular investment. Indeed, there is paperwork here from your solicitors attesting to the soundness of it. What has happened in the last few days that all of this would change?"

Despair crashed over him, and he fought not to panic. The last few days, being away from Miss Perry, had thrown some truths Abe's way. That is what happened. Truths that he liked her. Missed her. Cared for her far above anyone ever in his life. That he'd just come from her bed, where for the first time in his life he'd lost control, allowed himself to enjoy, to savor the woman in his arms told him all he needed to know about how much his situation had changed.

He loved her.

Fuck!

"The documents were forged. They were forged at my instruction. It was a mistake, I grant you, and I had not thought that Miss Perry had proceeded with the investment yet. I just came from her home, where she divulged this information. Of course, hence why I'm here before you trying to fix my error. Trying to stop the payment."

Mr. Turner stood, leaning over his desk. "There is no stopping it now. It is done, my lord and now I shall have the displeasure of telling my client that due to a lord's folly she has lost one third of her inheritance." The older gentleman, as stout as he was, seemed to grow in size at his anger. "How dare you play her the fool in such a way? Such funds may be nothing to you, but they are everything for others. Please leave, I have work to do, one particular job of telling Miss Perry that you've led her on a merry dance for reasons only you understand. I highly doubt that she will be so understanding. Good day to you."

Abe wouldn't normally let anyone speak down to him in such a way, but today he deserved the set down. Deserved to be called the bastard that he was—the scoundrel.

There was no coming back from this. Willow would never forgive him and he'd never forgive himself.

CHAPTER 14

$\mathcal{A}$ week after being told by her solicitor that her investment had failed, Willow sat in her library, having spent the past half hour pacing up and down the long room. Lord Ryley was due to arrive any moment. The mere thought of him made her blood boil, and she was ready to see him again after denying him these past days.

Thirty thousand pounds. She clutched her stomach, knowing she would never get that money back. Never have that security again in her life. What if she had risked all her inheritance? Not that she would be so foolhardy, but what if she had been interested in doing such a thing? She would've lost everything. Her home. The security for her friends who lived with her.

The bastard!

A quick rap sounded on the door, and her butler opened it, announcing Lord Ryley. His lordship stepped into the room, his hair, as usual, sat displaced atop his head as if someone had run their hands through it. His superfine coat fit him like her kid-leather gloves, and his

Hessian boots were polished to such a shine that Willow could see his lordships reflection in them.

"Please leave the door open, Thomas."

Lord Ryley schooled his features at her decree and came to stand on the opposite side of her desk. Willow gestured for him to sit before she also sat, adjusting the papers on her desk lest she stand, go about the desk and murder him in her library.

"Willow, I have wanted to see you. To explain. To–"

"There is no reason to explain, my lord. I understand perfectly well. You played me a fool and the green lass that I am, I fell for it. I should not have trusted you." Not just in the financial kind of way, but emotional as well. She'd given herself to this man. Allowed him liberties that she should never have allowed anyone. Not unless that anyone was her husband.

He sighed, running his hand through his hair. From the looks of it, he'd been doing that quite a lot today. Was he remorseful? She hoped so. If he was at least, it would show some kind of heart beat inside that chest of his.

"I'm sorry, Willow. I had not thought that you had already approved the investment. When you told me that you had, I did try to correct the action. As you know," he said, glancing down at his hands. "I was too late."

"Yes, well, when we spoke of it at the house party, I did not think I would need further tutoring on the idea. That you approved it, stated to the fact that you would be investing in the mine also, I had no reason for concern. What I did not know, of course, is that you were using me as a means of revenge."

He met her eyes, and she read the confusion in his dark, fickle gaze. "Who said that to you?"

"Lord Herbert explained there was some sort of

scandal involving your mother that forced her to leave England. That in some way you blame Lord Herbert's family and my own for her departure."

"Lord Perfect has no idea what he's talking about." Lord Ryley narrowed his eyes, contemplating her. "Did he tell you that his mother slandered my mother? Her best friend at the time. Called her all types of vicious lies simply because she was from Spain and not all peaches and cream as they so like their ladies of the upper ten thousand to be."

Willow took in this information and tried to tally it up with what Lord Herbert had told her. It did not make any sense. "That is not what he said at all. He told me that your mother left London due to having an affair with a man, not her husband."

"That isn't what happened at all, and I would suggest, madam, that you only speak the truth when it comes to my family. Unless you too are tainted as a liar like Lord Perfect."

"Very well," she said, leaning back in her chair. "Tell me your version of the events." Not that she deserved any of his treatment, his need to bring her down financially. Another part of her worried that he'd also set out to take her virginity to ruin her reputation as well. Not that he could hurt her any longer. She had ensured her future was secure before today.

"Lady Herbert disliked that my mother was regarded in the *ton* more highly than she was, especially since she was an outsider. A foreigner. They were friends once, yes, but that soon came to an end when jealousy imbedded its claws into Lady Herbert's spine. My mother was taunted and teased out of London and has not returned. I was left to be raised by staff and nannies before being sent off to school. Father fell ill at her leaving and never recovered. I place all of that dreadful time in my life at Lord Perfect's family and yours as well."

She shook her head, staring at him with pity. "Please explain to me how my family is involved?"

"Your aunt, Viscountess Vance, was in the thick of all this scandal. Throwing her opinionated self into the fray."

Realization struck Willow, and she stared at Lord Ryley with far greater insight. "And so you, all those years later, set out to ruin me financially because of something that my aunt did to your mother twenty years ago?" She barked out a laugh, unable to hold it in any longer. "You're mad!"

❧

Most definitely, he was mad. He was also shamed. Hearing Willow tell him that he'd taken revenge on her for something that happened twenty years ago made him look petty and idiotic. "They made my mother's life hell."

"Your mother now. Is she happy?"

He adjusted his seat, knowing his answer would make him look further like a fool. "She remarried a wealthy merchant in Spain several years ago. They are both very happy."

"And yet here you were, brooding and just waiting for your chance to strike like a Spanish viper." She leaned forward on the desk, watching him. Something in his chest hurt at the sight of her pain at her displeasure of him. He didn't want her to feel that way about him. At first, he'd wanted her to pay, but that had long changed. Had he known that she was going to move forward with the investment without further consultation with him, he would never have allowed it.

He loved her. For the first time in his life, his heart had beat outside of his chest for another. He wanted her to be his wife, but that right now seemed like a dream that would not come true. She hated him. Loathed him. He could see it in the blue depths of her eyes. He'd disappointed her.

"I'm sorry, Willow. I have hated them all for so long that I could not see past my hate. I should never have involved you in my scheme, but your aunt had been so cruel, so vindictive to my mother that I could not let it go. I was orphaned because of them all."

"No you were not, my lord. You were orphaned because your mother chose to leave you here in England instead of taking you to Spain. I do not know what story to believe, that your mother had an affair or if she was degraded by society due to the color of her skin, but either way, you choose to make me suffer for a crime that I wasn't part of. How could you do that?"

"The more I learned about you, the more time we spent together, I knew that I could not do what I had planned. Had you not moved forward on this investment, had you waited for our meeting, this would never have happened."

Willow gasped, and Abe cringed, knowing what he'd just stated was the wrong thing.

"Now you dare blame me for this? You're the one who gave me the investment, spouting on about how sound it was. How dare you blame me for your own scheme?" She stood, leaning over her desk. "I think you should leave, Lord Ryley. We have nothing further to say to one another."

He stood, coming to the desk and drinking her in, fear

and panic rioting within him that his error could cost him her. "I can give you the money back, Willow. It's nothing to me."

She scoffed, shaking her head. "Of course it's nothing to you. You have multiple properties, a business that due to men's greed and need to sleep with women other than their wives, you'll always have an income. That money that my aunt gave to me was all I had. Was all I'd ever have from anyone. It keeps me safe and allows me to keep my friends safe from vultures like you, gentlemen like you who think some women are worthy of marriage and others are only worthy of lying on their backs.

"You and your hatred stole thirty thousand pounds." The disgust on her visage was as sharp as a physical blow to his gut. "You can give it back? How very fortunate you are that you have the luxury."

"Willow, please," he begged, uncertain of how to make this right. Damn it all to hell. He'd been a bastard. A fool, and now he'd gone and broken what they had been progressing toward.

A future.

"You should also know that I have been asked by Lord Herbert to be his wife, and I have agreed."

This time the air did whoosh from his lungs, and he clasped the desk to steady himself, hoping what he'd heard was untrue. "What?"

"I'm going to be married," she said, matter-of-factly, walking about the desk and going to stand at the door. "Good day to you, Lord Ryley."

He stared down at the mahogany wood, his fingers clenched, and fought to think, fought to understand how he could fix this. Change all that had happened the last week. He closed his eyes, forcing calm through his blood.

Turning, he strode to the door. "Is that what you want?" he asked, hoping, praying that she'd say no. That she wanted him and not Lord Perfect.

"Let me answer this another way, my lord. I certainly do not want anyone I cannot trust and who would use me as a pawn for their own gain." She stared him down, cold and aloof. He'd never seen Willow so distant, and he hated the fact that he'd made her so. He'd made her like this toward him after all they had shared. Their bodies and their minds.

"Willow, please." He would beg if need be. He could not lose her.

"Leave. Now."

A footman appeared in the foyer, opening the front door. Abe glanced in the direction and spotted the very bastard who'd ruined his future, Lord Perfect, stroll into the foyer. Who was Abe fooling? He'd ruined his future. He'd pushed her away, used her, and made her lose a great deal of her fortune.

He had no one to blame but himself. Abe strode past Lord Perfect, the gentleman's lofty and amused greeting lost on him. It took all his effort not to look back. Not to run back to Willow and beg her to change her mind. To forgive him.

Instead, he crossed the threshold and strode to his carriage. Lord Ryley, The Spanish Scoundrel, never looked back. Not for anyone or anything. Not even his heart that he feared he'd left in the library of Miss Willow Perry's Hanover square home, Mayfair.

hree weeks passed, and he'd not seen Willow. The time dragged like an endless clock that never turned the full face of the hour, merely clicked and taunted that he would not move forward. He'd buggered everything up with the one woman who'd captured his heart.

He leaned back in his chair in his study, a glass of brandy in his hand on the armrest. He swirled the amber liquid, lost in thoughts of her. Was she happy? The talk about town was that the wedding plans were going ahead with great gusto. Invitations had been dispatched. Not that he'd been invited, but he knew from the Duke of Whitstone who had been.

There had to be something that he could do to win her back. His treatment of her, his immovable stance on revenge had clouded his mind, and before he'd known the damage he would cause by acting against her, it was too late.

A knock sounded on his door, and he bellowed to be left alone before the door swung wide.

Light footsteps sounded, and he glanced over his shoulder, a small slither of hope piercing his heart that it may be Willow come to see him. Instead, the sight that filled his view left him grappling for words.

"Mother?" he said, standing and going to greet her. "What are you doing in London?"

She kissed his cheeks, clasping his face, just like she used to when he was a child. "I came to try and amend your mistake that I heard from Lady Herbert that you've done."

"What?" he frowned, taken aback. "Lady Herbert. What on earth is she writing to you about?"

"Well, as luck would have it, I've been traveling and was in Paris when I received her letter last week. She was concerned that her son, whom you like to refer to as Lord Perfect I hear, is marrying a Miss Willow Perry. A woman that has apparently caught the attention of the renowned rake and Spanish Scoundrel, Lord Ryley. You." She gave him a knowing look, stepping past him to seat herself on the settee. "A glass of sherry, if you please and then come join me."

Abe did as she bade, taking in his parent whom he'd not seen for several years. She was as beautiful as he remembered her as a child, tall, dark-haired, and golden-skinned as he was. Even at her advancing age, she was a beautiful woman and one who had not deserved the treatment that she received. Which meant her correspondence with Lady Herbert made no sense.

He handed her a glass of sherry, sitting across from her. Abe leaned back in his wingback chair, wanting to give an impression of being undisturbed, but it was false. His mother being in contact with Lady Herbert after all these years was not what he'd ever expected her to say.

"Why are you here, Mother? You swore never to return to London after what was done to you."

She sighed, taking a small sip of her drink. "It is time that you knew the truth of my leaving England, why I fled as I did."

"The truth? But you were shunned out of London due to being Spanish. Lady Herbert and Lady Vance mocked and ridiculed you."

"They did, you're right, but they did so on my behest. I needed a scandal so bad, so degrading that your father would force me to leave. And so, I, along with my two closest friends, came up with a plan. They would shun me, make up lies of my infidelity, and mock my heritage. It was the only way I would've survived, Abraham. Had I not left when I did, I would not be here with you now."

"What!" Anger coursed through him at the thought of his mother lying to him all those years. Of hating people that were now innocent of the crimes he threw at their head. The thought that he'd treated Lord Perfect the way he had since Eton, the way he'd ensured Willow had lost her money was all based on a lie made his stomach churn. "Tell me everything."

His mother stared at the burning wood in the fire, quiet a moment. "I married your father for love. We met when he was on a grand tour and visiting Spain. We married abroad and returned to England. You know all this of course. Not long after, we found out we were expecting you, and I was so happy. I had a husband I loved and a child on the way. I had friends, and life was marvelous for a time, but then it all changed. Your father became surly and mean at times. Little things would set him off, and I was at a loss as to why."

His mother stared at the sherry in her hand, lost in the

past as she recounted the story to him. One that he was struggling to comprehend.

"Your father had syphilis, Abraham, and yet he expected me to remain a true and loving wife. I could not do such a thing. Had I stayed, I too would have succumbed to the disease. I tried to reason with him, explain the risks that I would be taking should I remain a true wife, but he would not listen. He wanted me to stay, and he wanted his nightly pursuits in the bowels of London to continue as well. That is when Lady Herbert and Viscountess Vance helped me plan. My only regret was that your father refused to allow me to take you with me. Decided instead that you would be better off with a nanny until you could be sent to Eton."

"And so you left me here, alone, all those years. Allowed me to be raised by servants since father had washed his hands of me. Why did you not return after his death?"

"Your father ensured I was unable to return. For my silence on his affliction, I had to remain in Spain. Should I not do as he decreed, he threatened to never allow me to see you again. He promised that you would travel to Spain when you were fourteen and you did." His mother leaned forward, clasping his hand. "I wanted to take you with me, but you were the future Marquess Ryley, and your place was here in England. My friends have kept me abreast of your life, and antics within the *ton*," she said, looking down her nose at him. "But from afar, just as I was made to live apart from your life. So you see, my dear, there was a reason for my banishment, just not the one you believed. Now that your father has passed, and you're a man, you deserved to know the truth. Especially when that truth is stopping you from marrying a woman, I believe, who has captured your heart."

The mention of Willow filled him with regret, and he stared at his mother, unable to believe this tale that she told. Everything that he thought was the truth, the reason his mother had left him had not been because of Lady Herbert or Viscountess Vance, but because of his father. Because his father had gone mad with the venereal disease, had threatened his mother with the same affliction.

Anyone in that situation would flee or try to escape. Abe stared at his parent and read the fear in her dark-brown eyes that he would shun her. Hate her for lying, but he could not. He reached across the space separating them and clasped her hand. "I understand, Mother. I just wish that it hadn't been so for you. That father was true to you and never fell ill such as he did. Lady Herbert and Viscountess Vance were true friends in creating a scandal so bad that Father banished you. I suppose I owe them thanks instead of loathing, such as I've shown them. It seems I owe many apologies." One to Miss Willow Perry the most pressing of all.

He shook his head at his actions. However would he make amends, but then, he had not known the truth either, so mayhap forgiveness will be forthcoming from all he'd loathed for so long.

"Why, however, was Lady Herbert writing to you regarding her son's betrothal to Miss Perry? From all accounts, her ladyship is pleased with the union."

"Oh, she's pleased and adores Miss Perry, but she doesn't believe her son is marrying the woman he loves. He was enamored if you recall some years ago to Miss White. They were not permitted to marry as her father wanted her to be a duchess. She is now a widow and will soon be returning to town. Lady Herbert believes that when her son sees her again, his feelings for her will be as strong as they ever were. That he'll regret marriage to Miss Perry, and the union will decline because of his mistake."

Abe couldn't imagine ever regretting a marriage to Willow. The idea no longer scared him or made him want to cast up his accounts, but instead filled him with longing. With a need to move forward, have a fuller, richer life. With Willow.

"Does Lord Herbert know that his first love is a widow and returning to town?"

"He does," his mother said, standing and going to pour herself another glass of sherry. "But he's in denial, and you, my dear son, are reported to be as well. In denial about your feelings for Miss Perry, if you need clarification. When I heard of the predicament that you both were in, I knew I had to leave Paris and travel to London. Tell you myself that you must make Miss Perry cry off her engagement to Lord Herbert and soon. Lady Herbert tells me she believes this would be the best for everyone. We may be getting older, but we still see things as clear as air, and I trust my friend. She thinks you're in love with Willow, and she believes her son is in love with the Duchess of Markson. The solution is simple. Now you must make it a reality."

Make it a reality. As simple as that. Abe wasn't so sure. Willow was extremely unhappy with him and rightfully so. He'd acted a cad, a bastard to have made her lose thirty thousand pounds. He would be hard-pressed to forgive anyone such a crime.

"I will try and make amends, Mother. I cannot say that I'm not disappointed in you in not telling me the truth sooner, years ago, in fact. Why did you not?" he asked, needing to know.

She shrugged, coming to stand before the fire. "There was little point. You may have disliked Lady Herbert and Viscountess Vance, but they knew the truth and were willing to accept your anger at them if it meant that your father's secret was kept just that. No one in London knows that he was ill with that disease, and no one ever need know. All of that is in the past, and other than the woman you love marrying another, there really isn't a lot to repair."

Abe shook his head at his mother's trivializing of the situation. It was just like her too. Face a problem and find a solution. Pity her solution to her problem years before had led him down a road of revenge and hatred.

"I will make it right and save both Miss Perry and Lord Perfect from marrying each other. I shall not fail in this."

"Good," his mother said, smiling at him. He smiled back. Even with all that had passed between them, the time apart and the reasons why, both true and false, having his mother home in England made him happy. And now he needed one other thing in his life to make him complete.

Willow.

CHAPTER 16

*W*illow threw herself into balls and parties, nights at the theater with Lord Herbert. Every time she was with him, she marveled at his kindness, his understanding, but each time it became more and more prevalent that she did not love him.

She liked him very much. There wasn't a lot not to like about the gentleman, but he didn't make her heart race. Not even when on a carriage ride home from the theater, he'd taken her in his arms and kissed her again. Properly this time.

For all his ability, she may have been kissing the back of her hand for all the emotion it brought up inside of her. The streets of London passed the carriage windows, and she absently stared at nothing at all, wondering if this is how her life would be from now on. An endless parade of social gatherings and very little else in between.

"Willow, are you happy?" Evie asked, staring across from her in the carriage.

She rallied and schooled her features, knowing that what she was about to say was a lie. Since Lord Ryley, Abe,

156

had left her library the month before, she'd slowly sunk into a life of lies. She smiled and danced, laughed, and allowed Lord Herbert to court her, plan their intertwined future. All the while her mind had been occupied with another. The scoundrel who had not only stolen her money but her heart.

"I'm very happy," she said, forcing the words through her lying lips. She bit back a sigh, wondering what Lord Ryley was doing at this very moment. He was probably at his club, women begging for any scrap of attention he may offer them.

Bastard.

Evie leaned forward, clasping her hand. Willow refused to look at her lest she see in her eyes that she was anything but joyful at the moment. For all of Lord Ryley's unforgivable actions, she missed him. Missed how he made her feel.

"You're lying, Willow. It's as clear to me as if I were looking through glass. What is wrong? Tell me. I'll not tell anyone else if that is what you wish."

Willow closed her eyes, slumping back on the leather squabs. "I'm not in love with Lord Herbert."

Evie nodded consolingly, her eyes full of understanding. "I know you're not, but I suppose you must decide if you're willing to let love grow between you in time, or not." Evie threw her a searching look. "Does your having concerns for your impending marriage have anything to do with Lord Ryley?"

The mention of his name sent a bolt of longing through her, and she bit the inside of her lip to stop her eyes smarting with tears. He didn't deserve any more of those from her. She'd cried enough over the loss of him. Over the fact he'd used her, seduced her into trusting him so he could steal from her and her security.

"I hate that man. Do not mention him again." She didn't need any more assistance in remembering his every touch, how his voice sounded deep and seductive against her ear. How his kisses left her longing and spiraling out of control.

"You love him," Evie stated matter-of-factly. "Even after his treatment of you, you love him still. You will need to decide if you're willing to walk away from a future with Lord Herbert, who is everything you've always wanted. A nice, secure marriage to a man who adores you. A future where children will feature. Safe and secure just as you wanted. Against a future with Lord Ryley. A man hell bound, riddled with debauchery and someone I've concluded for some time that is as much in love with you as you are with him."

Willow gasped, looking up to meet Evie's eyes. "He doesn't love me. His actions toward me are proof of that."

"Yes, while I agree he acted in a way that begs the question as to whether he is intelligent, we also must not forget that his calling on you the day before you learned of his ulterior action was to dissuade you of the investment. He was going to right the wrong he intended you."

"Little good that did. I had already moved forward with the investment."

Evie came and sat beside her, turning to face her. "And knowing that he tried to stop the transaction by going to your solicitor. Mr. Turner told you that himself."

"Whose side are you on? You're supposed to be my friend, not supporting Lord Ryley." Willow cringed at her accusatory tone. Evie didn't deserve her annoyance, which should be fully focused on Lord Ryley and no one else. And herself for that matter. For allowing her disappointment and wretchedness over his actions toward her to cloud her judgment and agree to Lord Herbert's proposal the moment he made it.

"Willow, you know that I'm on your side, but I also have watched you these past weeks, and you're not yourself."

Willow exhaled, her lips set into a thin line. "What does that mean? I have been myself and I'm perfectly happy with my choice." Even though she was not. Evie was right, of course, but she'd given her word to Lord Herbert. To cry off from the betrothal now would be a scandal she'd never recover from. Her wedding attire was being made as they sat in the carriage on their way to the York's ball. Lord Herbert's mother had hundreds of guests attending their church wedding before hosting them an opulent wedding breakfast at their London estate.

Not to mention Lord Ryley had been noticeably absent from any social events the last month. Was what Evie said true, and somewhere in that dark soul of his he cared for her? One would think that if that were the case, he would try to win her back. Try to see her again and ask for forgiveness.

Not that she would give him any such thing. Fiend.

"No you have not, and as your friend, I'm going to tell you the truth, even if you do not wish to hear it. You're in love with Lord Ryley, and he is in love with you. Perhaps you both have not admitted as much to yourselves, but when we were at Hampton it was obvious to us all."

Willow scoffed, adjusting her seat as the carriage started to slow before Lord and Lady York's townhouse.

"Scoff all you like, Willow, but he made a mistake, a dreadful one, but is that error worth a life of misery, of half truths with a man you do not care for. A life half-lived because deep down, you'll know you married the wrong man."

The carriage rocked to a halt, and without waiting for the footman, Willow threw the door open and jumped from the equipage. Evie followed at a more sedate pace, but Willow needed time to think, to clear her head. Panic clutched at her skin. Her hands clammy and hot within the confines of her gloves. Damn her friend for being so honest. She didn't want to know what others thought. What others believed Lord Ryley thought of her.

None of it mattered. She was engaged to be married to Lord Herbert. Lord Ryley had stolen from her. He didn't deserve anything from her other than her disgust forever and a day.

By the time they arrived at the ballroom doors, and they had greeted their hosts, Willow forgave Evie enough to walk into the multitude of guests to make their way across the room to where they could see Ava and the Duke of Whitstone.

Ava stood beside the duke, her arm entwined with him and a knowing, loving smile on her friend's face as she spoke up to her husband, who had an equally adoring visage toward his wife. Something inside Willow snapped, and tears pricked her eyes.

She couldn't do it. She couldn't marry Lord Herbert and only be half the wife she longed to be. He deserved a marriage of affection, of adoration, not a marriage made up of half truths.

Willow deserved the same.

She kissed the duchess as they joined their friends, greeting the duke warmly, but her smile slipped as she caught sight of Lord Ryley across the room, a woman on his arm she'd not seen before. They were in deep conversation with a group of friends about them, ignorant of her presence.

"Never mind Lord Ryley," Ava said, looking at her with concern. A characteristic that all her friends were adopting toward her these past weeks. One that had started to irritate Willow. No matter that their intention was good. "He'll not disturb you tonight. He wouldn't dare."

"He may do whatever he likes. It's no concern of mine," she said, raising her chin and taking in who else was present. Lady Herbert was here she could see, along with Hallie and Lord Duncannon, who were talking to some of their friends farther along the room.

Evie held out a glass of champagne to Willow, and she took it, her mouth parched and in desperate need of fortitude.

As much as she tried, her attention kept snapping back to the one spot in the room it should not. Lord Ryley was busy with his friends, laughing and discussing something that interested him, which most certainly was not her.

His lack of awareness of her was telling. Evie was wrong. He'd never cared and never would. She was missing a man who never really existed. While she'd always known he was a rake, he'd been sweet, intense, and patient with her. But it was all a front—a lie. The whole time he'd been plotting her downfall, loathing her for her relatives and their actions toward his mother.

Lord Herbert may not be the man she would marry, but nor would Lord Ryley. In time her heart would heal, and it would bloom once again, ready to love, to give over to someone else.

Her skin prickled in awareness, and she looked up and caught the eye of Lord Ryley, his dark, heated gaze pinning her to her spot. Her heart gave a lurch, and no matter how much she knew she should look away, ignore him, she could not. All that they shared, the many kisses, his seductive words as he took her on the daybed bombarded her mind, and she bit her lip, hating that he could make her want him as much as he ever did. He'd tried to ruin her. Had made her lose a third of her fortune.

Still, she wanted him. Wanted him with a need that overshadowed everything she knew of the man and knowledge of what he did.

His gaze didn't leave her, not even when Lord Herbert bowed before her, kissing her hand and pulling her onto the floor for a waltz. And damn herself, for the simpleton she was, she didn't want Lord Ryley to look at anyone, unless that anyone, that someone, was her.

$\approx$

*A*be watched Willow glide onto the floor with Lord Perfect, anger thrumming through his veins at the sight of it. It had taken him several weeks to accept the fact that she was to marry another. The whole of London was abuzz with the news and details of the forthcoming nuptials between the two.

He'd only attended tonight to see for himself that it was true. That they were a couple and he had lost her. It would seem so if her adoring gaze up at Lord Perfect and his, in turn, was anything to go by.

"Is that her?" Marigold said at his side. She clasped his arm, pulling his gaze away from Willow.

"Yes, it is her," he said, meeting his cousin's eye. She was his father's younger brother's daughter, an heiress like so many here this evening, but Marigold was sweet, pure and kind. The opposite to Abe. Perhaps that is why they had always been close. He'd spent many weeks at his uncle's estate when he wasn't in school after his father died and his mother was in Spain. She had heard the rumors that he'd been slighted by Miss Perry and had come to check on him immediately.

Abe was still trying to find out how that rumor had started. The Spanish Scoundrel did not get slighted by the opposite sex, and he'd not let the rumor stand.

"She's very beautiful."

He nodded once, clamping his jaw. "Well, we have arrived and seen for ourselves that she is indeed happy with her choice. Shall we leave?"

"What? No," Marigold said, patting his arm. "You need to speak to her. Just to be sure this is what she wants, for it's as plain as day to me that it's not what you want."

He scowled down at his insightful relative. "I've never wanted to marry anyone. You know that." His mother's words to win Willow back reverberated in his mind, and he cast a glance in her direction. She was so lovely tonight. Her red, silk gown accentuating her unblemished skin and slight frame. So tall and luscious. Kind to a fault. Should she want him, he knew he didn't deserve her. Only a great man should have such an honor. He was not a great man.

"You're in love with her. The Spanish Scoundrel does not attend balls and parties just to look in on a woman to ensure she was indeed betrothed. You never cared for all this fanfare in any case. Since I've known you, you have turned your back on society, loathed and ridiculed its fickle ways. You promised your mother you'd try to repair this wrong. Here is your chance. Tonight."

Abe noted Lord Perfect's hand dipped low on Willow's back. He knew how that skin felt beneath his fingers. The warmth, the softness. Anger spiked through his veins and he fisted his hands at his sides. "I need a drink," he said, leaving his cousin and striding off in search of a good, hard whiskey or scotch, anything would do if it blinded him to the sight of Willow waltzing with a man, any man, if that man was not him.

CHAPTER 17

*W*illow excused herself after supper and went in search of the retiring room. After completing her tribulations, she sat for a time in the empty, opulent room and calmed her heart. Not because she had been dancing and laughing all evening with her betrothed, who really was a very sweet man, but because another was present. The very person that she'd sworn to forget, to curse forever.

But she could not. No sooner could she do those things than she could push away her friends. She cared for him. More than he deserved, but that didn't mean that she had to forgive him. How could she forgive him for his actions toward her? An innocent in all things relating to his mother, and he'd punished her for other people's sins.

It wasn't fair in the least.

Willow sighed and stood, starting back toward the ball-room. The house was large, and she turned down a passage, stopping halfway when the location didn't appear familiar to the one she walked through to get to the retiring room.

"Lost, Miss Perry?" a deep, husky voice said from a shadowed doorway farther along.

She lifted her chin, facing down Lord Ryley. "As a matter of fact, I am. Not that it is any of your business."

"I forgot to tell you the last time I saw you congratulations. You must forgive me my forgetting my manners at the time. I was confounded, to say the least."

She scoffed, not believing that for a moment. "You? Confounded?" She strolled up to where he stood, noting his cravat was untied and hanging loosely about his neck. Had he just finished a clandestine meeting with the woman he'd brought to the ball? Had he just taken her in the darkened room behind him? Her stomach rolled at the thought, and she took a calming breath to stop herself casting up her accounts all over his shining Hessians.

"How are the wedding preparations coming along? Your grand match is all that London is talking about."

Willow knew that as well as anyone, and the pressure now to go through with the marriage was immense. Even though, deep down, she knew she could not. Lord Herbert was not whom she wanted. The blasted fiend before her was.

"Very well, thank you. Thomas has been very involved."

A muscle worked in his jaw and not for anything could she tear her eyes from him. Her gaze slid to his lips, lips that she'd dreamed about, longed to feel against hers, and she cursed herself a fool. What woman lusted after a man who had set out to ruin her? To bring her low financially and perhaps socially as well. Not that he'd made it known to anyone that they had lain together.

"Thomas?" He cleared his throat. "I suppose it is only expected that you would call him by his given name."

Willow met Abe's gaze, wondering why such a thing would aggravate him if his caustic tone were any indication. "He's to be my husband," she lied, knowing she'd flee London—England—even before she went through with such a future. Not that Lord Ryley needed to know that. The scoundrel.

"Hmm," he said noncommittedly. "I suppose you would." He turned and went into the room behind him and left her standing in the passage.

For a second, she debated turning about and fleeing his presence, but the need to see him more, to hear his voice, if only to disagree with him forced her hand, and she stepped into the room.

He stood beside an unlit fire, leaning on the mantel and staring at the fire that had been set, ready for tomorrow. "Where is your lady friend?" Willow asked, having expected to see her dressing or fixing her hair at the very least.

He glanced at her curiously, a small frown between his brows before he chuckled. "Are you suggesting I was in here having a tryst with the woman that I brought to the ball?" He strode over to a decanter of whiskey and poured himself a glass, downing it in one go. "Sorry to disappoint you, my dear, but that is my cousin recently returned to town. I simply accompanied her as she wished."

Willow refused to allow the relief pouring through her to amend her features. She held fast to her face of impassivity.

"Why do you ask about my affairs in any case, Miss Perry? You're to be married, am I not allowed to court whomever I please, like you? Move on from our little incident in Hampton such as it was and the one again in London."

"You may do whatever you want, just as you always have," she said, reminding him of his scheme all along to ruin her. And he had ruined her in a way. Certainly, no one else lived up to him now or made her feel an ounce of the emotion that she always felt when around Abe. The urge to stomp her foot at having to have fallen for a man who was so wrong for her in so many ways. He'd wanted to make her pay, damn it.

Which he succeeded in doing, a little voice mocked in her head.

Willow ground her teeth, coming farther into the room. "I was surprised to see you here, that is all. Even accompanying your cousin as you say, you've not been in society the past month. I thought you would've scuttled back to your hell hole you love so much." Irritation tore through her at his treatment of her. Of his plan to bring her down. How dare he? How dare he make her care for him while all the while wanting nothing more than to make her pay?

"Oh, I've been in my hell hole as you state, my dear. Still," he shrugged, "I have been part of this society longer than you, and whether I like the lifestyle or not, the people in this ballroom are my friends and keep Hell's Gate profitable. It never hurts to show interest, even when I do not have any. It is the same for women who warm my bed. They're all the same. After a tumble...before they fuck you over."

Willow gasped. Did he mean her? "Are you implying that I used you, my lord? That I gave myself to you only to marry another?" She could not have heard what he'd just said. Surely he was simply baiting her.

"Isn't that what you have done, Miss Perry? Or have I been mistaken this past month?"

Willow stormed over to him, standing nose to nose with

the vexing, impossible man. "You sought revenge and used me while working toward your goal. If anyone pushed me into the arms of another it was you. Why don't you just admit it, Lord Ryley? You're jealous. You're so jealous that someone other than yourself can call me their own. Maybe what everyone is saying about you is true."

"And what truth is that," he said, his voice low with a dangerous edge to it that made her shiver. She was walking a delicate line with Lord Ryley. He wasn't tamed, and certainly wasn't a gentleman most of the time. There was no telling what would happen if she kept poking his temper.

"That you love me. That you regret pushing me into an investment that took a third of my money. That you want me still." Just as she wanted him. After all that he'd done to her, still her body yearned for his touch. If only he'd admit his wrong. Admit that he was sorry. To beg for forgiveness.

His lordship on his knees, begging for mercy, would be a lovely sight.

"You want me to admit to wanting you?" he said, stepping toward her and pushing her back against the small table that ran behind the settee.

"And everything else," she whispered, the backs of her thighs hitting the table. His intoxicating scent of spirits, of sandalwood and something else altogether, lewdness perhaps, consumed her and heat pooled at her core.

"Oh, I want you. I want you on your back right here and now." He scooped up her gown, pushing it up her legs so the cool night air kissed her skin. "I want you to break off your engagement to Lord Perfect. I want you to be mine."

She should stop him. Shove him away. But she did not. Silly, silly woman that she was. His nearness consumed her, and then what he'd said, his words, flittered through her mind. He wanted her for himself? She was engaged, and this was wrong. For all that Lord Ryley thought of Lord Herbert, he did not deserve for his fiancée to be kissing another man.

And that is exactly where this interlude with Lord Ryley would end if she did not leave right now.

With all the self-will she possessed, Willow pushed Abe away, stepping out of his reach. "I should not be here, and you should not be trying to seduce me."

"Why ever not? I want you as much as I ever did. You cannot marry Lord Perfect. You do not care for him, Willow. I can see that you do not, and all of London knows it as well."

All of London knew that she did not care for her betrothed? Heat bloomed on her cheeks, and she took a calming breath, reminding herself Lord Ryley wasn't always correct about things. "What do you know of feelings, Lord Ryley when you care for nothing but yourself?"

"That isn't true. I care for you. More than I ever wanted to or thought I could, but I do."

"What?" she asked, turning to face him. Never had she thought to ever hear such words from the Spanish Scoundrel. The way he looked at her, sincere and as if his future hung on her response, made something in her chest twist.

He cared for her?

Dare she hope that his feelings ran deeper still, to love? For as true as she was standing before him, she loved him. Loved that he vexed and teased her. Loved him enough to overlook his stubbornness and foolhardy schemes. She could understand the reasoning behind it. Had she known her mother at all, she would never have wanted her run out of London simply because of her ethnicity.

She would have fought back as well and sought to make those who had hurt her family pay.

Her aunt had been one of those people, and although Lord Ryley's revenge was misplaced, there was honor pushing him forward to seek it.

"I owe you an apology, Willow. I owe Lord Herbert one as well. There are things that I was not aware of that have come to light and have consequently changed my opinion on things."

Willow took a step toward him, needing to know what had changed. "How so?"

"Come," he said, taking her hand and leading her to sit on the settee beside him. The muffled sound of a cotillion drifted around them, and only the candles burning in the passage illuminated the room. The sitting room was dark and private and dangerous. She should not stay. She should leave, return to her betrothed, and tell Lord Ryley to call on her tomorrow and explain himself.

Instead, Willow sat, turning to face him and drinking in his exquisite visage that looked at her with emotions she could only dream would last forever.

"My mother is in London. She arrived several days ago, and with her arrival, so too came the truth."

Willow frowned, wondering what that could mean. "What truth?"

"Well, as to that," he said, explaining to her everything he had learned.

She sat and listened as Abe told her of his mother's plight all those years before. Why she was made to leave without her son, and the reasons why she could not return. The more she listened, the more Willow realized that Abe

171

had been living under a miscomprehension. One that his mother should have told him the truth of years ago.

"Did your mother know of your plan to seek revenge when the opportunity arose?"

"No," he said, sighing and leaning back in the settee. "She knew my dislike of her friends, or enemies as I assumed it was the case, but because I simply ignored their existence, there was little concern on her part. She was in Paris when Lady Herbert wrote to her and asked for assistance."

"Lady Herbert. What? Why was Lady Herbert requesting assistance?" Willow asked, sitting forward. A wedge of dread knotted in her stomach, and her mind raced as to why her ladyship was asking such a thing.

"She believes that your betrothed is not in love with you. That he's in love with another. She wrote to my mother because she believed that you also did not love her son. That you, in fact, loved Lady Ryley's son instead. And so, a marriage between Lord Herbert and Miss Perry would be a disaster if it proceeded."

Willow stared at Abe, unable to take in all that he was saying. "But Lady Herbert has been so very helpful with the wedding plans. She's so excited."

"Of course she would be, Willow. You're a perfect woman that any man would be proud to marry. I know I would be."

She blew out a breath, meeting his dark, hooded eyes that burned with a need that echoed her own. "You don't want a wife, Lord Ryley. You made that abundantly clear, and should I marry you, I would not like to share."

He chuckled, leaning forward and taking her face in his hands. Willow could feel herself falling for his charm. He only had to touch her, and she was lost. No longer in control.

"The last month has been hell, and I've come to realize that I don't want anyone else in my life other than you. You are the sweetest, most honest and most loyal woman I've ever met, and somewhere between seeing you in breeches at my club, or beneath me on a daybed here in London, I fell in love with you. I love you. I want you to break off your understanding with Lord Herbert and marry me. Be mine."

Willow sucked in a shaky breath. Her hands fisted about the lapels of his coat, and she realized sometime during his speech, she'd reached for him. The idea of being his filled her and a sense of peace settled upon her. The feeling that this was right coursed in her every nerve.

"You're certain that Lady Herbert will not be devastated if I cry off? Lord Herbert has been very attentive."

Abe's eyes narrowed, his face becoming hard. "The blaggard has kissed you again, hasn't he?"

Willow grinned, unable to stem a small chuckle at his annoyance. "They were nothing like your kisses, my lord. I may as well have been kissing my hand."

He scowled at her a moment before he audibly sighed. "I suppose one must kiss one's betrothed. It would be strange not to."

Willow shuffled closer to his person, wrapping her arms about his neck. The scent of sandalwood intoxicated her senses, and for the first time in weeks, she felt herself again. Alive and happy. So very happy. "Do you have anything that you'd like to ask me, Abraham?" she teased, wanting him to say what she'd longed to hear from almost the moment she knew he was an unattainable rake.

He closed the space between them, kissing her softly on the lips, leaning his forehead against hers. "Marry me?"

She nodded, tears pricking her eyes and making the vision, the perfect lovely, unforgettable vision of him, blur before her. "I will marry you. I promise to love you always. To be faithful and honest and forever yours."

"I do too," he said, kissing her again, this time, no sweet, short embrace, but a kiss that fired her blood and made her wish she'd closed the door when entering the room. But there would be more of these to come. Tonight merely marked the beginning of their life. Their start of forever.

EPILOGUE

Four months later

illow sank into her bath before the roaring fire at Blackwood Hall, Abe's ancestral home, and where they had moved to after their wedding in London, a week after she cried off from marrying Lord Herbert.

As Abe had said, Lord Herbert seemed more relieved than devastated that she wanted to end their understanding, and only today, they had returned to Blackwood after attending Lord Herbert's wedding to Her Grace, the Duchess of Markson. The woman he should have always married had the bride's father not been set on her marrying a duke and not an earl all those years before.

Willow lay back in the jasmine-scented water, closing her eyes, her hand moving to touch the small, hard swelling on her stomach that wasn't noticeable to anyone but her. Now that they were home for the foreseeable future, certainly through the winter months, Willow would tell Abe of the child. She had snuck away in London to

their doctor and had her prognosis confirmed. With everything well, she felt ready to let Abe know that he was going
to be a father.

The crackling fire warmed her arm as she lay it on the
side of the tub. Emotion welled up inside her, and she
could not remember ever being so happy. She was married
to a man she adored, her friends living happily in her
townhouse in London where she had asked them to remain
after she married Abe. Neither of them wanted to move
back to the country, and the house would otherwise be
empty. It was a perfect solution to have her friends there.
Hallie was still in town and promised to keep them out of
trouble.

Willow smiled at the thought of Evie and Molly, the
last of their friends who were yet to marry. She felt certain
they too would meet the men who would sweep them off
their feet. Next season she would ensure they were courted
and adored and married by Season's end.

"Well, this is a delicious sight if ever there was one."

Willow chuckled but did not move. The water soothed
her aching muscles after all the traveling they completed
that day. "How were the tenant farms? Everything in
order?"

"Everything is well. My steward has it under control as
usual."

Willow opened one eye when she heard a rustling
beside the tub. She sat up as a muscular, hairy leg stepped
into the tub, followed by another. She gasped as he sat and
joined her, water toppling over the sides and splashing on
the Aubusson rug.

"Abe, the mess!"

He grinned, shrugging. "It'll dry," he said, reaching out
and pulling her over to his side. Instead of laying on him,

DARE TO BE SCANDALOUS

like she so often did when they bathed together, she strad-
dled his legs, placing her aching core against his manhood.

The water made him slippery, and she clutched his
shoulders, running her hands over his chest that would
forever catch her attention. From the moment she'd agreed
to become his wife, he'd bathed her in love. Sometimes to
the point that she worried about him should anything
happen to her. Whether he would be okay, so deep was his
affection for her.

His mother had stayed on in London and had taken
her place back within the *ton*, which made Abe happy. As
for his club, he still ran the establishment, but it had
changed to a men's only club, become less *demimonde* and
more *beau monde*.

His wicked gaze made her forget everything else, and
she leaned forward, kissing him, taking from him whatever
she wanted. Over the last few months, she'd become quite
bold in her seductions of him, enjoyed teasing him
throughout the day, and making him wait.

Today had been no different. Throughout the carriage
ride home, she'd thrown him hot little glances that
promised pleasure. His tongue meshed with hers, and she
sucked on his, mimicking what she liked to do with his
hardened member.

Abe groaned, his hands a vise about her head, keeping
her against him. She reveled in his passion, taking all that
he offered and matching it twofold. Willow undulated
against him, his hard, large member sending spikes of
pleasure to radiate through her body.

"God, I love you," he said, kissing his way down her
face, her neck, before lifting her a little to take one erect
nipple into his mouth. His tongue flicked out, teasing the
bud, and she watched him, her breath ragged. Willow bit

her lip, grinning at what his touch did to her. Made her feel.

So much joy. So much love.

"Your breasts are so perfect." His hand ran over her other breast, his thumb and forefinger rolling her nipple. Willow moaned, rocking against him as his mouth teased her flesh.

"You're not to come yet, my love."

And then she was lifted and spun about in the tub. His large, muscular arms sliding down hers to set them against the edge of the bath. On her knees, Willow looked over her shoulder, wondering what he was up to. His body leaned against her back, his cock settling between her aching folds, and realization dawned.

They had never made love this way. Was it even possible?

He kissed her back, slipping her hair over one shoulder. His tongue traced her spine, and Willow closed her eyes, unsure she could take much more of his teasing. It was delicious and all-consuming.

"Stop taunting me, Abe," she gasped as he slid against her core again, just enough to keep her wanting more. And she'd never get enough of her husband, that was one thing she was certain.

❧

*A*be would never get enough of Willow. She was his world, and he adored every little tidbit of her. His balls were tight, his cock hard. Her heat slid around him as he teased them both. He groaned at the delicious friction, wrapping his arms about her to clasp her breasts.

They hung heavy in his hands, and he tweaked her nipples, eliciting a sweet gasp of need from her lips.

He reached for his cock, guiding himself into her, taking her inch by sweet inch until he lodged himself fully. Her tight core clamped about him, and he thrust hard once to tease her.

She moaned, undulating her ass, seeking his cock, and he sucked in a breath, not wanting this to end. Damn, she made him want. Always a need that was never sated, no matter how much they came together in such a way. From the moment they'd married, it had been like this, and he hoped it would never end.

He adored her and only lived to make her happy.

She was wet, coating his cock even in the water, and he thrust again, picking up his pace. They hadn't had sex like this before, but he was certain she would enjoy it. If her moans and sweet little gasps were anything to go by, she was enjoying his tupping of her from behind quite a lot.

Abe leaned back, clasping her hips and thrusting hard and deep. With one hand he reached around, sliding it against her cunny and teasing her little nubbin that he loved to suckle, to kiss and lick. Later, he promised himself. Next he would bring her to release on his face.

The thought of the act made him harder still, and he groaned.

"Oh Abe," she gasped, reaching down to place her hand on his, holding him against her mons.

Her sexual demands only excited him more, and he continued his relentless pace, knowing how she liked to be fucked hard and fast. Deep and sure. His cock swelled as he took her. Leaning down, he kissed her neck, the sensitive, sweet spot under her ear.

She mewled, gasping, and then he felt it. The tightening, pulling sensation around his prick. Her release spiked his, and he joined her in the kaleidoscope of pleasure, taking her until at last she relaxed in his arms, sated and satisfied.

He disengaged and helped her to slip about to face him. He held her against his chest, his hand idly running up and down her back. Her skin was so soft and smelled always of flowers. Today it would seem the water had been spiked with jasmine. A scent he now forever associated with her.

"That was different," she said, turning a little to kiss his chest before she placed her hand over his heart, one finger idly playing with his chest. "I liked it."

He liked it too. He kissed her temple, holding her close. "I thought you might, and I have other things planned for you this evening. Other enjoyable delights that I know you'll enjoy."

"Hmm," she mumbled, meeting his gaze. "I'll look forward to it, and speaking of other things for this evening. I wanted to tell you something."

"You do?" He glanced down at her expectantly. "What is it?"

"Well," she said, sitting up a little to see him more clearly. "When we were in London this week, I went to the doctor."

"Are you well? Is there anything the matter?" he said, interrupting her and sitting up so fast that water sloshed onto the floor once again. The poor maids would be cursing them later for this mess. His hands searched her body as if he would find something ominous, and Willow clasped them, holding them still.

"Nothing is wrong, Abe. Everything is perfect, in fact."

"It is? Then why did you need to consult a doctor?"

She didn't reply, merely grinned at him, and waited for him to understand. To know what she wanted to tell him. It only took a moment, and his eyes widened, his mouth gaping for words that wouldn't come.

"We're going to have a baby. I'm pregnant."

"Damn it," he said, clasping her shoulders.

For a moment, Willow wasn't sure what to say. Was he happy or did *damn it* mean he was disappointed? "You're not pleased?" she asked when he merely stared at her like a stone statue they had in certain parts of the garden.

"Oh no, I'm more than happy, Willow. I'm beyond all thought and coherent sentences, but I'm beyond happy."

Tears blurred her vision, and taking one hand, she slid it to cover the small bump that sat low on her belly. "The doctor thinks I'm several weeks along. Do you think it's going to be a girl or a boy?"

Abe let out a half laugh, half snort. "I hope it's a girl. I'd love to have a daughter who is as sweet, as pure, and good as her mama."

Pleasure filled her at his words. Such poetry she could get used to. "I'd like a boy so that he can grow up as handsome and noble as you."

"The Spanish Scoundrel. Would you want a son knowing his father held that title?"

Willow reached up, running her hand over his jaw, knowing how much the title irked him once they were married. Some still referred to him like that, and he loathed the connotations that came with the name. "I fell in love with the Spanish Scoundrel, and you were not so very bad. Personally, I think your reputation was exaggerated more than necessary."

"Really?" he said, one eyebrow arched.

Heat pooled between her legs at his wicked glance that

181

promised retribution for saying such a thing. He stood in the bath, more water splashing to the floor. Willow looked at him with exasperation before he lifted her up, hoisted her in his arms, and stepped from the tub.

"Not so very bad, you say?" he said, only a few short strides to the bed. He hoisted her onto the mattress, and Willow laughed as she bounced. "We shall see about that."

Willow reached for him as he came down upon her, a willing recipient for anything that Abe, the Spanish Scoundrel, was willing to do to her. Not just tonight, but always.

For all days.

Dear Reader,

Thank you for taking the time to read *Dare to be Scandalous*! I hope you enjoyed the third book in my League of Unweddable Gentlemen series. I admit this is my favourite of the series so far. I love a dark, brooding, hot hero. As it would seem my heroine did also!!

I'm forever grateful to my readers, so if you're able, I would appreciate an honest review of *Dare to be Scandalous*. As they say, feed an author, leave a review!

Tamara Gill

TO BE WICKED WITH YOU

LEAGUE OF UNWEDDABLE GENTLEMEN,
BOOK 4

Evie Milton knows she'll never marry. But that doesn't mean she can't celebrate her sister's betrothal to Finlay Stone, Duke of Carlisle. Until the bride-to-be runs off with the wrong man, that is. Now, if they have any hope of avoiding a devastating scandal, Evie and Finlay will need to bring the runaway bride to heel. And Evie will have to somehow ignore her growing attraction to the handsome duke who can never be hers …

. . .

In order to avoid disinheritance, Finlay needs a wife, and he requires one now. Finding a match wasn't terribly difficult. Keeping her, however, was another story. Going after the chit was his last option. What he never expected was how he'd start to feel for Evie. She's beautiful, kind, mature...and an entirely unsuitable bride. If only he could convince his heart of that ...

All it takes is one spontaneous kiss to scatter their best intentions to the wind. But as secrets emerge and truths are revealed, can Evie and Finlay find their way to happily ever after—or is their wicked liaison doomed to end in heartbreak?

LORDS OF LONDON SERIES
AVAILABLE NOW!

Dive into these charming historical romances! In this six-book series, Darcy seduces a virginal duke, Cecilia's world collides with a roguish marquess, Katherine strikes a deal with an unlucky earl and Lizzy sets out to conquer a very wicked Viscount. These stories plus more adventures in the Lords of London series! Available now through Amazon or read free with KindleUnlimited.

KISS THE WALLFLOWER SERIES
AVAILABLE NOW!

If the roguish Lords of London are not for you and wall-flowers are more your cup of tea, this is the series for you. My Kiss the Wallflower series, are linked through friendship and family in this four-book series. You can grab a copy on Amazon or read free through KindleUnlimited.

TO MADDEN A MARQUESS

TO TEMPT AN EARL

TO VEX A VISCOUNT

TO DARE A DUCHESS

TO MARRY A MARCHIONESS

LORDS OF LONDON - BOOKS 1-3 BUNDLE

LORDS OF LONDON - BOOKS 4-6 BUNDLE

To Marry a Rogue Series

ONLY AN EARL WILL DO

ONLY A DUKE WILL DO

ONLY A VISCOUNT WILL DO

ONLY A MARQUESS WILL DO

ONLY A LADY WILL DO

A Time Traveler's Highland Love Series

TO CONQUER A SCOT

TO SAVE A SAVAGE SCOT

TO WIN A HIGHLAND SCOT

Time Travel Romance

DEFIANT SURRENDER

A STOLEN SEASON

Scandalous London Series

A GENTLEMAN'S PROMISE

A CAPTAIN'S ORDER

A MARRIAGE MADE IN MAYFAIR

SCANDALOUS LONDON - BOOKS 1-3 BUNDLE

High Seas & High Stakes Series
HIS LADY SMUGGLER
HER GENTLEMAN PIRATE
HIGH SEAS & HIGH STAKES - BOOKS 1-2 BUNDLE

Daughters Of The Gods Series
BANISHED-GUARDIAN-FALLEN
DAUGHTERS OF THE GODS - BOOKS 1-3 BUNDLE

Stand Alone Books
TO SIN WITH SCANDAL
OUTLAWS

ABOUT THE AUTHOR

Tamara is an Australian author who grew up in an old mining town in country South Australia, where her love of history was founded. So much so, she made her darling husband travel to the UK for their honeymoon, where she dragged him from one historical monument and castle to another.

A mother of three, her two little gentlemen in the making, a future lady (she hopes) and a part-time job keep her busy in the real world, but whenever she gets a moment's peace she loves to write romance novels in an array of genres, including regency, medieval and time travel.

www.tamaragill.com
tamaragillauthor@gmail.com

Made in the USA
Coppell, TX
04 February 2021

49347574R00109